WOOD SPIRIT

a new england horror story

By

Johanna Frappier

To Leo J. Frappier

— MASTER PLOTTER —

without whom, this book wouldn't exist.

Chapter 1

Richard Wanker despised a lot of things. He would never forgive his mother for marrying Terrence Wanker, the man who took off and left them destitute in this cow-crap Vermont town that only barely managed to be more pathetic than Peachtree, Vermont. Jeepers crow, this was the *90s* and they still didn't have cable, she still hung their clothes out to dry on a clothesline, and they still used a rotary phone. He would never forgive her for naming him Richard Wanker, which naturally made his name 'Dick' Wanker when he hit the fifth grade. Now, even though he had graduated and they were supposed to be all grown up, he still wanted to bash the hell out of every single smug face at Our Lady of the Lake High School. Even though this was the reality of Richard's humiliating life, he actually did not feel spiteful tonight on this most glorious of evenings — what with the full moon shining over the trees, and the mission that lay ahead. Two months back, he had met a girl at the prom. She was a friend of a friend and she had a huge rack. They were so big, they ballooned into one awesome unit. Her name was Marie and she liked really cool stuff like The Cure and skateboarding. He skated sometimes, at the ramps out behind the library and he told her he'd take her there sometime. Well, even though it had been two months since the prom, she still called him! She had even called him today. Someone must have told her by now that his last name was Wanker — but still, she called him, and she wasn't even ugly. He could hardly believe his luck.

He was making good time. He was supposed to meet her in her back yard just after nine. They had to sneak because her parents were Nazis — her words, not his. He was walking down Old Crabapple Road, which was one of the original cow paths that cut straight through his town and into Peachtree, where Marie lived. Even though they had slapped some pavement on the road, it didn't really bring it into this century. It was narrow and bumpy with huge trees growing right on the edge that hung their branches low over the middle. When they got ice storms, Old Crabapple could be inaccessible for weeks, littered with massive broken branches that had cracked under the weight of the ice. Hiking paths and deer paths — and deer paths that were used by hikers — crisscrossed the road like ant trails. They never put any lights on the road either, so it was pretty dark, but Richard didn't mind. The full moon lit everything up very nicely, and he was a night hunter, so he could easily get around without getting lost or pissing himself over noises in the woods.

Like the noises he was hearing right now, and had been hearing for some time — as if something was following him. It sounded like feet or hooves pressing into the soft,

3

pine-needled forest floor. Sometimes the steps were just a whisper of sound and sometimes the animal stepped on a twig and made a loud crack that shot through the still night. At first he thought it was a curious deer that was trailing him, but the sound of the footfall wasn't right — a deer would be lighter. Sometimes the footfall sounded human, but no, the gait was wrong. It was probably some freaken' huge stag, or Bobo the circus bear had escaped and was dancing around on his hind feet. What else could it be? He wished he had his gun. That thought made him smirk — hunting on the way to Marie's house like he was bringing them dinner. He beat his fist to his chest, "Me man! Me bring meat for meal!"

The footsteps behind him changed direction and sounded like they were coming out of the woods right at him. He spun around. "What the fuck?" He strained to see what was coming out of the woods. All was silent. Whatever it was had stopped advancing. He caught a whiff of something rank. Something dead.

He reached down and swiped some stones off of the road, hawked a loogie, then ran full-sprint towards the spot where he thought the animal had stopped. He'd pelt it a couple of times and send it scampering back to its bed. He stood very still in the spot where the animal should have been. He couldn't make out which direction it had gone. He hadn't actually heard it run off — the blood pounding in his ears had covered any sound the animal might have made. He circled in place and kept a sharp eye. He listened. Not only could he not hear the thing anymore, he couldn't hear *anything*. No peep frogs or critters in the underbrush, not even the blasted cicadas that always went on and on in the heat like chainsaws. He slapped at a mosquito that landed in his ear. He turned again and heard his nose crack just as his face exploded in pain. He was lifted off his feet and thrown down to the ground, where his head smacked against a rock and made the hollow sound of a spanked cantaloupe. He scrambled to get up, but something was holding him down.

A thick fluid seeped down into his eyes just as his brain registered the sight of a tall, emaciated man with a gaunt face covered in what looked like onion skin over his skull. He tried to scream, but only grunts and groans escaped his mouth that no one could have heard — had someone been there. He suddenly felt a searing heat on the left side of his head, but didn't realize it meant that his ear had been ripped off. He wondered why he couldn't reach up to soothe the hot spot, but didn't realize his arm had been yanked off. He opened his mouth to scream again, but a leathery piece of something was suddenly there, sitting heavy on his tongue and making him gag. In his last moments he regretted giving his mother trouble about his name. He wished she was there, holding him and telling him that he was having a nightmare.

The creature took its ear out of Richard's mouth and stared at it as he held it in his yellow fingernails. He touched the scabby place where his ear had been, then dropped it and bent to chew at Richard's stomach.

Chapter 2

Yeah, I got a story for you. Back in the 90s, this mayor from Peachtree, Vermont, called me up. He either didn't think about the time difference between our locations, or he didn't care. Either way, he woke me from my beauty sleep. I was on my mattress, an old stained futon bit, with my sweet and supple bedmate. I describe her as sweet and supple because her name currently eludes me. Okay, it eluded me then, too. I was in a tequila coma when the phone started ringing. That phone almost never rang, and the pounding in my head confused me, so at first, I had no idea what was going on. I jumped up and danced around yelling,

"Wha? Wha?" like it was a four-alarm fire bell. To further confound me, my friend rolled to her side, stunning me with an alpine view of skin that smoothed down from her shoulder, to her waist, then jutted up again to her pointy pelvis. She tugged the pillow over her head and moved no more. The phone continued to ring. Dry desert air blew through the window that was propped open with a paint stirrer. I could tell by the purple fire in the sky that it was too-early-o'clock. Between rings, the neighbor's chickens squawked and scrapped in the dirt out front.

Who was calling? My number was found in special ads in special magazines in unique places where people like my mother never ventured. She lived in blissful oblivion, where the understanding was that my "religion" required phonelessness. Cults equaled freedom from nagging mothers; I don't know why more people didn't think of this.

"Hello."

"Yes, hello. Is this Sebastian Park?"

9

"Yup." I winced — I could smell my upper lip. "Kinda early for business." I glanced at my watch-free wrist.

"I'm sorry, sir. Is it?"

"Yut. It's only..." I leaned across the naked woman and pulled at her limp-noodle arm — she didn't have a watch either.

"Sir, I'm using my best judgment, you'll understand, as you don't have your hours listed in your ad." The man on the other end of the line cleared his throat.

"Aw, it's all right." I rubbed at my face and scratched my scalp, which was loaded with sand or some other unidentified grainy stuff. Whatever it was — I really needed a shower. "How can I help you today?"

"Do you really hunt ghosts?"

I found something in my nose. Good God, I thought it must have been lodged there for more than a year — it was hard as sun-baked brick. "Why yes, Sir. I am indefatigable, always au fait on the latest technique, and ever sagacious, and have a vade mecum of appurtenances in appreciable amounts." Most of the time *I* didn't even know what I was saying, but you could always count on the client to swallow those big words quietly. I scratched my balls and sighed. If this call went well, I'd be working tomorrow and therefore would have to hunt for clean underwear today.

The man's discomfort continued to pour out through the phone and into my small, minimally-furnished room. I could hear him as he shifted around over there at the other end of the line and swallowed repeatedly. I was used to this — people needing me, but not wanting to need me and feeling entirely ridiculous in their need. I gave the man a moment before asking, "And who are you, sir?"

"I am the mayor of Peachtree, Vermont."

I tucked my chin in my neck, my eyebrows shot up — I never had a mayor call me before. Would they be paying me from the town coffers? Would I get the best room in town? Would there be a parade — an apple pie, at least? I grinned and tried to decide how long *this* job would take, but I was unable to come up with a number. My giddiness set my nerves a-jangle. "What kind of apparition you got there, mayor?"

***

They wouldn't pay for a plane ticket, which incensed me a tad, but I didn't let it show. I would just make damn sure this was a particularly strenuous case, resulting in lots of overtime. I wondered in whose bed I'd be spending my overtime — a buxom blonde in L.L. Bean hiking boots? A blueberry-pancake-making housewife yearning for a cowboy from New Mexico? Depending on the housewife — I could be a cowboy. These amorous thoughts kept my spirits light as I sped in my trusty black Volkswagen Bug from the desert sepia of New Mexico towards the green of the East Coast.

I left my friend back at the ranch, with the bedroom window open in case she couldn't find the door. I made a new friend, a third-shift clerk at a gas station in Indiana. Our eyes locked over the Twinkies and Mentos and there was no turning back. Miss Indiana taught me how to say, "Shut up and lay back," in Spanish and I taught her how to scream like a tea whistle. She told me that she liked my strapping physique and mane of Kennedyesque hair. They all do. I'm not bragging — that's just the way it is. I was born with this body and face that woman get excited about. I'm what you'd call 'man-pretty.'

I arrived at Peachtree, Vermont about four days after the mayor's phone call, in need of yet another shower on account that I could still smell Miss Indiana's ghastly L'Air Du Temps wafting from my nethers. My Bug was littered with Burger King wrappers, Hershey wrappers, condom wrappers, gum wrappers and clothes wrappers since I had to do some shopping along the way — it's quicker than the Laundromat. I brought nothing with me when I left the house except for my 'equipment' which amounts to nothing

13

more than a metal detector and a blender with a balloon on it. Around dawn, Miss Indiana found the equipment and wanted to use it in a foul manner. Regrettably, I asked her to go into the station and get us some Twinkies and burnt coffee for breakfast. As soon as she was in the shop, I ran my fingers through my luxurious and oily mane and raced off. I didn't want to be too late for work.

About twenty minutes before the Peachtree town line, I made my last convenience store stop. The place was called The Black Chicken and it was one of those glossy franchise outfits with overpriced fruit and dusty condoms. The bell ting-a-linged when I sauntered inside, and lo and behold, you should have seen the gorgeous filly that they had cooped up in there. This girl, with her long, raven hair, boots with feathers, and lush, wise-cracking mouth was a firecracker ready to blow. She was talking to some hunched-over redhead who may or may not have been pretty - I couldn't tell, what with her goth-posturing and hair curtain covering her face. The one with the black hair, though — yowzers — seemed like too much for even me to handle, was talking about breast implants and her future at the local strip club. I'll tell you what, I adore convenience stores – you can never tire of the entertainment the people in those places can provide. I truly hated to leave that girl, but I promised I'd be back. I think I've wandered in my telling here, so....

Just over the Peachtree line, I found a river running parallel to the road. I unfolded myself from the car seat with much complaint from my bones. I found an old dry-cleaning bag underneath the passenger seat, along with a can of Lysol. I shoved every big and little bit of debris I could find in the dry-cleaning bag, then threw the trash in the trunk with a mental note to find a dumpster later. I got my small toiletry bag from the glove compartment and a duffle bag from the trunk, then sprayed the entire car with Lysol, slammed the door, windows up, as if I had set off a bug bomb. I had to give it time to work and not return to the car for at least

15

twenty minutes. I hoped I hadn't let things go too far — that not one of the things that had taken up residency with me on the long trip was big enough to drive away with my prized car. This is no joke — I found a cockroach carcass the size of a hotdog when I was fishing under the seat for the Lysol.

I stomped through long grass and blood daisies to get to the river, where I undressed and dunked myself in the frigid water. It must have been in the eighties that August day. The air was thick and soupy, so the frigid mountain water felt fantastic. I know why people dunk themselves in the river to feel close to God. The experience always made me gaga. Extremely hot water was nice, too. I love the hot springs in New Mexico and the naked natives there, Bonnie and Heather, who like to rub my cramped muscles. Alas, there was no one around this river to rub me but an indifferent butterfly and loud blue jay. The water was deep enough for a swim, at least four feet, and this part of the river was tame as it rolled over big and small boulders. I splashed around a bit and enjoyed the shock of the water as it shrunk

my jewels to a still pretty impressive package. As the water

licked around my thighs I began to have impure thoughts of

a milkmaid come-a-skipping and a-jiggling through the

woods. But then, a sudden image broke into my thoughts, an

image born of being a man, naked in the woods, in the

middle of nowhere. Ghost banjos twanged out a duel. I

stopped my swooning with a strangled cry of disgust and was

pissed at myself for ruining a perfectly good fantasy. I

checked the far riverbank — no horny hunters there. No one

hanging around the Bug. It wasn't the first time I had been

afraid of being alone. One thing about being a pretty man,

the offers never stopped coming at you — from both sides.

And a third side too, now that I think of it — those repressed

men that claim they aren't gay...yee-haw, scary buggers.

Quickly, I fished in my travel kit for soap, shampoo,

toothpaste, and toothbrush. I put the toiletries on a mica-

filled rock that glinted in the sunshine, and hastily groomed myself while I kept a constant eye on my surroundings. By nature, I'm not a paranoid person, but I didn't feel alone in that river and I didn't like the feeling of whatever was near. I was totally out of my element — I loved being around people, so I could manipulate them into my pants or sell them something – but whatever was with me in the river that day wouldn't be impressed by my tricks. When I finished, I dressed quickly on the rocky shore. My new clothes were immaculate — pressed slacks, button-down shirt, finely-crafted leather belt, ostrich-skin boots the color of honey, and my sharp, white Stetson placed a-top my recently raked-through mane.

Back at the car, I opened the doors for final aeration and sat in the passenger seat. While I shaved with my battery-operated, I got the feeling that whatever was out in the river had followed me to the car and now sat in the back seat.

Okay, it's time for us to sit in a circle and talk about our truths. I'm a hack ghost hunter — I admit it — don't hire me. Now that we have that out of the way, I'll have you know my grandmother was an extremely sensitive woman who could sense the spiritual world. I loved that woman. I believe everything she told me. Every trick I use now, I learned from her reality.

So anyway, within half an hour, I appeared nothing like the slob I was before. I even changed the expression on my face from 'prowling insatiable' to 'friendly concern', so I could work on perfecting the appearance by the time I reached the Peachtree town hall. The problem was, 'friendly concern' hadn't been used in several months and it felt a little stiff on my face. I opened my mouth wide and moved my jaw up and down several times like a wooden puppet. In the end, I had to settle for 'happy and shrewd' as 'shrewd' appealed to my ego in a way 'concern' never could.

I rolled easily into town, following the very good directions given to me by the mayor, and pulled up to a slanted parking spot on the street before the ancient but festive town hall. It appeared like Peachtree celebrated Fourth of July every day, what with all the bunting and flags flapping in the breeze.

I got out of the car and turned around to look at the land I had traveled through. Peachtree was in the cleft of two mountains that shot up on either side. When I was driving into this small place, I was able to see the entire town spread out like an inspiration for motel art with its white-steepled church on a carpet of lush green, pastures dotted with grazing cows, and silver rivers.

I stretched my arms above my head, then trotted up the granite steps of the town hall. I had that queer feeling again, sharp as a physical force that stopped me abruptly between steps five and six. My face flamed in shame and I felt like I was in church without any pants on. And there were eyes on me, too — I felt them. I actually dipped my proud head for a moment before I caught myself, corrected my posture, and forced myself to walk through the doors with much put-on bravado. The truth was, I wanted to do an about-face and run back down those stairs, get in the Bug, and squeal out of town like a pig an hour before farmer's dinner. It was crazy — I had never once lost my cool since those long ago formative years when The Fonz and Dr. Ruth took hand in my making. I was bothered by the mere second of doubt that had moved up against me and left its mark like a physical blow.

The mayor was finishing with a meeting when I presented myself to his assistant, so I sat out my time on a straight-backed, tortuous bench that only the Puritans could have invented. I watched the mayor's assistant move about the office. She wore jeans and a beaded tunic, early forties, with pretty little manicured toes poking out of her leather sandals. She smiled at me while I watched her, and I smiled right back.

"Mr. Park, would you like to read about the history of Peachtree? I have a book here that traces us right back to when the English settlers met the Algonquin people who were thriving in this land. They thrived down the East Coast, for that matter...."

"Well, honey, that sounds fascinating, but I'll pass for now — from what I understand, I've got pressing work to do here.... So, are you married?"

She took her sweet time in answering. She put more papers in an ancient wooden file cabinet while her desk fan whirred back and forth.

I leaned back in the torturous Puritanical thing, and hoped I seemed relaxed and casual.

She moved to sit on the bench with me — the little coquette! My heart leapt to my throat — sweet Jesus — I thought we were going to start making out right there.

"Yes, I'm married. Very happily, as a matter of fact."
Her voice was warm; it tightened me all at once. There were
very fine lines around her mischievous eyes, laugh lines I
assumed, because now that I studied her glowing face, I was
almost sure she was younger than my original estimation.

"Does it matter?" I whispered — which I admit is
theatrical and way overdone, but I find that, in the field, that
the old standbys work rather well.

She patted my knee and asked how old I was. She
"Oooooed" loudly when I told her I was thirty-five.

"Well, Hun, I'm sixty-two tomorrow, and if I wasn't
married I would scoop you up right now and take you out to
dinner with my AARP discount!" She patted my knee again,
then shot off the bench to resume filing. "M-mmm." she laid
her eyes on me. "So handsome!"

I'm pretty sure I blanched, and I was still duh-faced
when the man I assumed was the mayor came gliding out of
his office, escorting another suited man. Both of the men

had to be in their sixties, or looked sixty and were actually over a hundred, like the broad singing "What a Wonderful World" over by the filing cabinet.

I scratched the back of my neck and leaned forward, my elbows resting on my knees while I waited for the mayor to send the other guy off. The mayor, his comrade, and the assistant were all in fabulous shape. When I say fabulous, I mean their clothes hung on them as if they were Sports Illustrated mannequins. Their skin, although showing some lines, was fresh and healthy-looking. Their eyes were bright and sharp. Every single person in that room was attractive. Sure, the mayor's hair was thinning, but that's all I could pin on him and it didn't even detract from his appearance.

This put me in a bit of a sour mood that was somewhat tricky to cover up, but cover up I had to — this was business. This was money to buy a new Bug, money to buy boxes of wine to pour into the gullets of vapid young women...I needed this job.

"Good Afternoon!" The mayor boomed as he strode forward, hand outstretched. He grasped my proffered hand and clapped my shoulder. "Say! You're a strapping thing! Don't get many of those from the outside, do we, Yvette."

"Nope." Yvette chirped while she continued to file.

Outside where? Outside the town hall? These people were odd. Not only were they breaking the rules by having fabulous physiques in Obese America, but they were standing up straight and saying weird things in a happy way and seeming to mean it.

Again — I admit — I was a bit put off. Up to this point in my life, it was relatively easy for me to walk into a room and command it with my confidence and toned tummy. Being on a more physically equal level with these people left me deflated. I followed the mayor into his office, hat in hand and ego lagging behind, like a whupped puppy.

We sat — he in his cracked leather chair on the other side of his desk, and me in a plush guest seat. He concentrated on me for a moment, sizing me up, I assume, then he clucked his tongue and reached to fiddle with a painted rock that rested on his blotter. "Shit."

I sat up straight.

"I can't sit here like this — I need to get some of this nervous energy out. You play Ping-Pong?"

When the client wanted something, especially when the client might hold big purse strings, the answer was always 'yes.' "Yes." Yay. Ping-Pong.

The mayor hopped up like a wily mountain goat and scooted over to the other side of the room to the Ping-Pong table. He rolled up his cuffs. I got a clear view of the gold Rolex on one arm and the gold anchor-chain of a bracelet on the other arm. He wiggled his eyebrows, "Ready?"

"Absolutely!" A headache started to form in my right eye — a needling headache that grew as I tried my best to entertain the mayor. I won't tell you I was any good at the game, but I wasn't *that* bad. After we went at it for about twenty minutes, the mayor's energy level seemed to reach equilibrium. He took a seat behind his desk and I sat in the chair across from him.

He began. "You know, I'll be honest with you, it wasn't my idea or to my liking that I called you in on this."

"I appreciate your honesty, sir." I stretched my legs out and crossed my ostrich boots at the ankle, relaxing a little at his admission. I did appreciate his honesty; it let me know he was uncomfortable with me — that's always good for something.

He picked up the rock. I could see what it said now — 'I love you Daddy,' in carefully painted strokes.

"You see, Mr. Park, we have here in Peachtree..." he scratched his neatly-trimmed sideburn and seemed greatly agitated, "...an...*entity* I guess...." Here he gestured with his hand, shaking his fingers, as if he wanted to cast the word 'entity' far away from him, "...and we'd like to get rid of it." The hand was reined in. He stared at me.

His stilted speech led me to believe the Ping-Pong match hadn't leveled him out much. "I see. Where is this entity?" I always used the same word the client used; it made them feel a measure of confidence in paying me to chase nothing — entity, spirit, ghost, poltergeist, apparition, shade, Casper — whatever they were most comfortable with.

The mayor looked at me from the corner of his eye. "The entity, Mr. Park, is not contained — it roams about the entire town." He sat forward and put both hands on his desk as if bracing himself. "Will that be a problem?"

'A problem?' *A problem?* Hell! My ego shot up from the floor and back into my head where it belonged. It took everything I had to keep from singing Hallelujah! I cleared my throat. "Not a problem, sir. I once had to trap an entity over the Pacific Ocean; (lie) I can tell you all about it right now whilst enlightening you on the intricacies of my equipment!" I served this line often to suits, as it made them twitchy and usually called meetings short. I wasn't disappointed.

"That's all right son, maybe some other time." He was no longer making eye contact. "Now, you'll be lodging in Roger Haversham's place. It's a B&B called The Ox Blood Inn. It's a very nice place; he does very well for himself. It's simple, but clean, and Roger is a fantastic cook — even did some time at the Sorbonne." He flapped a bunch of papers at me. "Here are the directions, a map of the town, and other bits of town info — history and such — that might help. Call me if you need me." He stood and offered his hand.

I shook his hand firmly and showed him all of my shiny white teeth — they cost me three exorcisms, at least. I hoped I could get a couple of weeks pay out of Peachtree without having to be accountable for my everyday actions. I could produce detailed fabrications when people called for them, but rule of thumb for life, love, and business — if possible — it's always best to keep your mouth shut.

When I stepped out of the town hall, a wave of nausea slimed right down my face and almost brought me to my knees. I gasped, bowed my back, and bent over. My arms quivered as I rested my hands on my knees. Across the street, on the town common, the green grass glowed. Children in blinding white romp clothes chased a bright red ball. Their mothers followed behind them with gorgeous silhouettes, hallelujah breasts, and hair that flowed like skeins of silk. I straightened up. One of the husbands waved to me. He was dressed like a dandy about to traipse off to the country club with his chums. Argyle. I shivered. Creepy. The place was a more than a little Stepfordy.

With one finger, I pulled at my collar, undid the top button of my shirt, and sat down on the granite step. Where in hell was I? I've been in old Victorian haunted houses, ancient brick haunted factories, haunted mines, and even affected RV's. What was this place, so like a dream it made me want to crawl someplace dark and small to hide? Inside my gorgeous mess of hair, I scratched at an old sore. I watched one of the mothers kneel down and stroke the cheek of her child. Mommy's dress plumed about her like ethereal light.

Suddenly, I was mildly frightened. Forcing myself to move, I stood straight, and walked stiffly to the Bug.

Chapter 3

I drove to The Ox Blood Inn. The B&B was actually painted ox-blood red. A small weathered plaque was screwed to the clapboard siding right beside the main entrance door. The sign proclaimed the house was built in 1789. I had to stoop to get through the doorway or risk getting beaned by a beam.

Roger was an immense man with fluffy gray hair. He wasn't so much fat as incredibly wide and tall — I bet he could frighten a lumberjack. He was so large you could hear his hinges grown as they suffered his mass. Around his legs twined his incredibly large cat — the biggest I had ever seen.

He told me it was a Maine Coon, but I'm pretty sure it was a bobcat. I smelled cat ass clear across the room. Rog stood waiting for me with an offering of chocolate chip cookies. I took the entire plate from him.

"Thank you, Sir."

He broke out into a booming, magnetic laugh, which worked like white magic to dispel the fright and shame that still clung to me like an infection.

"Come on, boy, I'll show you your room. You staying on for a time, that right?"

"Oh, most likely," I intoned with a bow of my head and a stern frown to show respect for the seriousness of the situation.

He narrowed his eyes and tilted his head. "Uh-huh. That's good to hear. As long as you get rid of it, then."

We climbed the stairs. All of the treads were sloped and the staircase was very narrow. Cat Ass sat at the bottom of the stairs with a puss on his face. He flicked his bushy gray tail. "What's up with your cat, Rog?"

He bent down and stroked the smelly thing. "Aw, he's got a bad hip. Hurts 'im to climb the stairs."

It seemed like Cat Ass was just too massive to climb the stairs, and he was ticked off that I was taking his daddy away from him. Rog gestured for me to follow him as he clambered down the narrow hallway. He bumped into a picture frame and knocked it off its nail, but caught it before it smashed to the floor. He grumbled, "Dangnabbit," and placed it back on its hook, then kept walking. He unlocked the second door on the left with a skeleton key — ambiance, he explained — and opened the door to a room that was small, but clean and bright. The walls were whitewashed over daub and the pine board floor was glossy. Sheer white curtains puffed in and out at the open window. A high mattress lay in a sleigh bed, and on the walls were pictures of mountains and daisies.

"Whoa, this is a beautiful room!" I took my Stetson off and placed it on the bed. "Hey, I saw that little bar downstairs — want to share a bottle of wine? It's on me!"

He rubbed his hands together. "Ooh! That's a good idea!" We went back down the creaky stairs and started in on the first of several bottles of Australian Shiraz and the plate of cookies.

"So what the hell is going on around here?" I clinked his glass to mine and snarfed down the red wine like it was life's blood. Cat Ass kept trying to rub on my legs. I kept kicking him away, incognito-like.

Rog shifted his derriere on his stool. His ass hung so far off both sides, I was afraid he'd lose the bar stool in his crack. "It's a strange thing, really – like a cloud that floats around town and doesn't blow away in the wind. I've seen it once myself and heard stories from lots of folks who have seen it."

"Oh — you've seen it yourself? Want to tell me about that?"

He frowned and rested his huge hands on his wide knees.

"Okay...you *don't* want to tell me about that...."

"No, it's not that I don't want to tell you...." He took a couple of gulps of wine. "It's just really disturbing, you know? There's a feeling that comes with seeing it. Once you've experienced this feeling...well, it's terrible — you just want to die. I really don't like talking about it." The color had left his cheeks. "It was last year about this time. I was out working in the shed, preparing the yard and the inn for a hurricane that was expected to hit us straight on. I thought I heard someone call my name. I thought it was my neighbor, Pamela Franklin, but that didn't make sense because Pamela has a hard time getting around. She's got a bad hip and she would have been outside only if I had helped her outside — which I didn't. Matter of fact, I was fetching the plywood I had bought to nail over her picture window. I could have sworn it was her voice — I heard a few more words, like 'go' or 'no' or something like that. I turned around and saw this cloud of smoke going away from me. I just looked at that thing and I wanted to cry myself. Jesus Christ, I tell you — it was horrible. And it's not smoke from a chimney...it stays low to the ground almost like it's walking. Yeah, it seemed like it was walking away from me. After that, I puked my guts out for almost a week." He looked at me. Hard. "You ever deal with anything like that? I mean, are you really ready for this shit?"

I slapped the bar. "Of course!" Cripes — walking black smoke! It was probably exhaust drifting over from some farting jalopy in the next town, something they of pristine Peachtree couldn't fathom.

Like Drunkenstein's Monster, I wobbled up to my room around 2 a.m. — the real witching hour — and used the walls to hold me up on the turns. I felt big in the little room.

Then I felt hurt when I crashed over my duffle bag and kissed the wooden floor. The spins came on right away — blasted tannins — so I decided the floor would be a great place to sleep, and quickly passed out. A persistent tapping noise at the window forced me to consciousness. I refused to look out there. Whether it was a tree branch scratching at the window, or a Salem's Lot freak — I didn't care. My red-wine head hurt and I was going the hell back to sleep. I dreamed that the tapping continued, so I got up and opened the window. There was a black ball out there, suspended before me and blocking the full moon. When I opened my mouth to gasp, the black ball squeezed into my mouth, filled my throat and landed like a bomb in my gut. I woke up again, pressed on the pain in my belly with both hands, and swore I would never consume that much red wine and cookies in one sitting ever again.

The next morning I set out to begin 'Peachtree Research,' morning number one. I drove to the center of town, parked in a slanted spot on the street in front of an antiques shop, and then roamed the quaint streets. It was a picturesque New England village with white clapboard shops where artists sold their paintings of the ocean and their silverwork of fairies and dragonflies. There was homemade soap and homemade cheese and pulled taffy. Hand-carved lighthouses and chain-sawed tree stumps that looked like bears. I headed for a small brick building on the corner, *Ma's Breakfast*, where people were lined up outside, waiting for a table. The smell of blueberry pancakes sizzling next to maple sausages made me want to weep. I excused myself as I wove through the crowd and searched for a seat. I found a single stool open at the counter. A sweet gal came over and poured my coffee. She was a tiny thing, pert, and smelled like griddle and honey. I stared at her. She bit her bottom lip as she stared back. I winked and pointed to the exit.

"Well, yeah, okay," she said, then ran her tongue over her teeth, "but I only got five minutes."

"That's okay, darlin'!"

"Hmmm, of course it is." She stepped back and checked out my butt as I sat on the stool. "Yeah, okay — I'll meet you out back in five minutes...by the wicked big oak tree...just beyond the Dumpster."

I clicked my tongue. "Gottcha." Then I watched her ass as she delivered orders — pumpkin muffins, barnyard omelets, corned-beef hash and fried eggs. When it was time to go, I took a napkin, found a pen on the counter, and wrote 'BE RIGHT BACK' then placed it on the counter under my coffee cup. I pushed my way through the crowd to get back outside. I went around the corner of the building and down a steep driveway. 'Rustic quaint' quickly gave way to 'business as usual' — the pavement was cracked, trash skirted the edges of the small employee parking area, and a scraggly alley cat hissed on cue. The landmark Dumpster seeped something foul and beyond it —nirvana — there was the promised oak tree.

40

When I strolled around the Dumpster, I found her leaning on the tree and fiddling with a pack of cigarettes.

"Do you mind — I only got five minutes...." She drew her pierced eyebrows together as she concentrated on getting her cigarette lit.

"Yeah, yeah — five minutes, I hear ya, Sweetheart." Under her black skirt she had full, firm thighs — sweet Jesus — like she was a smoking-hot, little gymnast. She was too short for what I had in mind, but luckily, the tree we were using had been severed long ago. It looked like it used to be a double tree, shaped like a 'V', but half of it didn't make it. The cut-off part served as a little step.

"Here, step up." My voice had gone husky at the thought of her and I rubbed her legs through her skirt as I turned her around. She lit her cigarette. I slid my hands up her thighs, and pushed the skirt to her waist. I had my pants around my knees in less than two experienced seconds and

41

just before I was about to slide home, I stopped and studied the woods behind us.

There it was again — that feeling that something was there, *watching me*. "Fuck," I hissed and forced myself to look away.

"Ah...yeah — please do." She withdrew her cigarette from where it hung in the corner of her mouth, clamped it with her fingers, then brought both hands above her head as she leaned against the tree. She tapped her watch and exhaled.

"Hey," I looked down to watch as I pumped her, "you know about this black cloud floating around town — the one people think is a ghost?"

She adjusted her ass cheek and brought the cigarette down to take another drag. "Honey, everyone knows about that. What turnip truck did you just fall off of?" She tightened up when we both heard a big 'boom' sound — the tightening was glorious. We relaxed when we realized it was a trash truck lowering a Dumpster at *Gary's Lobstas,* the shop next door.

"Shit, honey, now we have even less time — he's drivin' over here next." She groaned when I thrust faster. "Who are you?"

"I'm the ghost hunter that the town called in. I'm Sebastian Park." I spoke into her hair as I reached up to shake her finger. My eyes began to spin in my head.

"Angel! You back there?" The disgruntled voice came from the side of *Ma's Breakfast.*

"Shit — get off." Angel pushed away from the tree. She dragged her underwear up and shoved her skirt down, then moved her sweaty bangs off her forehead. "If you're going back inside, don't order the ham steak — it's questionable. And hey, remind me to give you my number." She flung her cigarette at my feet, kissed my cheek, and took off running.

I ground out the still-lit butt with the heel of my boot.
I felt eyes on me again. The sensation was so nerve-
wracking, that I actually couldn't turn around and bring
myself to check it out. Stiffly, I walked back up to the
restaurant. I returned to *Ma's Breakfast* for dinner, too.
Peachtree was a very small town and there weren't many
restaurant options. Angel and I bonded spiritually on our
second meeting — I helped her remove a splinter from one
apple-hard buttock. It was tricky, but any good citizen would
have helped the poor thing.

After she pulled her pants up, she reached up and
hugged me. "Honey, yer all right, you know that?"

Her cheeks were like dumplings — peach dumplings.
She smelled like the diner – like fried, sugary dough — and I
had the strongest urge to just open my mouth, and suck one
of those cheeks in and bite down, hard. I chucked her on the
chin. "Dumpling, you're too sweet."

Behind us, there was a rustling in the woods, followed by the most grating, high-pitched scream I have ever heard in my entire life. I grabbed her arm and jumped back two feet, almost yanking her off her stalks. My blood drained to my feet and I swayed to keep balance. "What the hell was that?"

Angel took her arm back and rubbed at her bicep. She winced as she dug in her apron pocket for her cigarettes. "Easy, Killer, it's just a fisher cat." She gave me a hard look. "And don't grab at me like that ever again – Mighty Ghost Hunter."

I snorted. "I've never met a ghost hunter that wasn't afraid, and I'm sorry; I didn't mean to grab you that hard." I held my arms out for a hug.

She rolled her eyes and lit her cigarette. "I gotta go."

"Hey, wait — what's a fisher cat, and Jesus, why would it scream like that? Really, that sounded like someone being murdered...." Suddenly, the scream came again, farther off, and spine-raking. I listened to it this time, and concentrated. It really sounded like a woman screaming into a microphone while she was being strangled. It totally sounded like every description of a banshee scream I've ever heard.

"You don't know what a fisher cat is? It's a freaken' nasty thing, like a weasel." She used her thumb to fiddle with her nose ring as she blew smoke through her nostrils. "Last year I saw one running up there," she pointed at the driveway we used to walk up to the diner, "...and it kind of runs sideways, right, with its back all hunched up." She shivered and started bouncing on the balls of her feet. "Well, last week, when I came in for the morning shift, I saw one of those fishers, dead, out in front of the diner." She chucked the butt to the ground and stomped on it with her too-big Doc Martin boot. "That night, this awful screaming starts in the woods, and now, it's been like that every night around this time. Just screams every five minutes for about an hour.

I guess it misses its mate. Someone should hunt it down and put it out of its flippin' misery."

"Remind me never to cry on your shoulder when a loved one dies." I took her hand. "Yeah, okay, let's get out of here. I really don't need to hear that again." As she walked in front of me up the drive, I watched her calves and planned on licking them without mercy on our next go-round.

***

Over the next few days, I didn't want to appear lackadaisical on the job, so I made a point of walking around town and trolling through people's backyards with any one of my various pieces of equipment bleeping and whirring. I handed in my first written report, which included my vague uneasiness in quite a few situations, and first-hand experiences from several people in town. All of their stories sounded just like Rog's story. The mayor didn't acknowledge my report, but he didn't fire me either. As for my true

impressions, I didn't know what they were talking about.

They sounded like a bunch of crazy people from a crazy

town. Mass hallucinaticn isn't an uncommon phenomenon.

I didn't see any smoke, never mind any *haunted* smoke.

Chapter 4

"Jessica, get my socks and put them in the box for me, will ya?"

Jessica didn't want to get Eddie's socks for him. She didn't want to put them in the box for him or pack any more of his shit for him, and now she was starting to think she didn't want to take off with him while he followed his rock n' roll dream, either. Sure, it all sounded good last week when they planned it. She didn't really have any family — she was just a wanderer that had come to Peachtree over a year ago and gotten a job at the big guy's inn. Mr. Haversham talked too much, but the work was okay. She met Eddie soon after she came to Peachtree, and at first, everything was great between them. They liked the same music, Thai food, old cartoons and screwed like pent-up inmates. Everything was perfect for a whole year. Then Eddie started talking about leaving and going to Vegas to be the next David Lee Roth, and well, it all started to get old.

She got up, got Eddie's socks and chucked them in the box on his twin bed. At least he was moving out of this rodent-ridden apartment that smelled like fish because he lived above a fish store. Maybe he would stop blaming her for the smell. She checked herself in the mirror and admired her blue eyes as she put on more black eyeliner. She imagined she looked like Gwen Stefani, but she actually favored Alice Cooper. She hoisted one Frankenstein boot onto the bureau and tucked the cash she had fished from his drawer into her striped knee-hi sock. Eddie would never find the money there; he never took off her shoes and socks to screw her anymore.

An hour later, they put the last of Eddie's stuff into the little U-haul trailer that they had rented and took off, pulling the thing with her Jeep. No one waved them off – it was just another Tuesday night. Five minutes later, on Old Crabapple Road, the rear right tire of the trailer blew out.

"What? Damnit!" Jessica hit the steering wheel and rolled her eyes at Eddie, who had already fallen asleep. "What the hell was that?" She already knew what it summed up to — dead tire. If this wasn't a sign that she shouldn't leave town, she didn't know what was.

Eddie rubbed his hand over his face. "Where are we?"

"Still in Peachtree, moron...." Jessica reached across him and opened his door. When she did, he tried to push her face into his crotch. She started slapping him and he started laughing. "Eddie! Cut it out! Get out and fix that tire!"

Eddie flipped the visor down and wiped at his smudged eyeliner. "Honey, I ain't never fixed a tire in my life. You go do it."

She folded her arms across her chest and bit her tongue to keep from crying. Then she threw her door open and stomped back to see about at the tire. She let the tears run free as she stared at the flattened tire and wondered how she had gotten into this mess. How had she ended up with Eddie? What did she ever see in him? How was it that she was twenty-two and just left a dead-end job to be homeless with a no-talent moron? She wondered how in the world she was going to change her life around. No home, no money, no skills....

The thing snatched her by her hair, twisted her head like a bottle cap and broke her spine clean, then tossed her behind a bush in less time than it takes to form a hamburger patty. It squatted down beside her body to eat.

When Jessica didn't get back into the Jeep for a good five minutes, Eddie shrugged and put on his headphones. He'd had his five-minute power nap, and now needed to listen to some tunes to get into the zone if he was going to jam a little at their next stop. He sat back and closed his eyes. He opened one eye. Where the hell was she? It was freaken' dark out there. He took off his headphones and pressed the stop button. And it was freaken' *quiet* out there. He pressed his nose against the window and took in the dark woods. He got out of the Jeep and walked around to the side of the trailer where Jessica should be fixing the flat tire. She wasn't there. Something reeked like grandpa's shit-riddled La-Z-Boy. He heard soft noises — a wet, squishing sound. It was coming from behind a big mess of bushes. He stood still as he stretched his neck up and tilted his head to see over the bushes. He couldn't make anything out. It was too dark. Weird shit started going through his mind. He backed up, walked slowly and quietly to the Jeep hitch. He wasn't stupid. It was pitch black out, Jessica was missing, he was hearing slurping noises, something wouldn't come out from behind that bush, and he had seen enough movies to know it was time to get out — quick. He gingerly pushed at the hitch.

He put more heft into his actions and strained to lift the hitch up. He fingered the metal tab thing. He didn't know how to get the trailer off — Jessica had had the U-haul guy hook it up. He kicked at the unit and swore under his breath.

He heard breathing. It was right behind him. He squawked, lunged forward, and tried to leap over the hitch, but he couldn't raise his feet high enough to go over it. He ran straight into it instead, effectively cracking one knee cap. The pain was beyond anything he had ever felt. As he fell to the ground, he held his leg and cried out. Then he saw the creature with its nose hanging off its face, as it limped towards him with its slack jaw and yellow eyes. He screamed ten times in quick succession when it reached for his Bon Jovi hair and dragged him into the woods. His screaming stopped when it clunked his head into a sizable oak.

Then it was able to eat in peace. When done, it scratched at the base of the oak like a cat digging in a sandbox. Working fast, it threw great loads of dirt between its legs, until the hole was large enough. The creature limped over to the pile of licked-clean bones and cradled them in long thin arms, then brought the bones back to the hole and dumped them in. Never blinking, it sniffed the air. It bent over and covered the bones with dirt using the same cat-like movements, then raised its head and screamed out a long wail.

Within an hour, a short, round man came whistling down Old Crabapple Road on his shiny new mountain bike. He took the front tire off the bike, put the bike in the back seat of the Jeep next to a box that had socks hanging out of it, got behind the wheel, and put the tire in the passenger seat with a pat. He drove off with the trailer gimping behind.

Chapter 5

I had been in Peachtree for a little over a week when, one morning, Rog found himself in a jam. At 6:30 a.m., he pounded at my door.

"Whadaya want?" I ground the heels of my hands into my eye sockets. Was he for real? "Jesus! What does *ghost hunter* mean to you? To me, it means that I work at night and *sleep* in the morning."

He yelled through the door. "It means you hide out all day, indulging yer tallywacker and fantasizing about your big paycheck. But I won't tell anyone if you come out here and help me right now."

There was a thud — I think it was his head against the door. I sighed. "Gimme five minutes." I heard a muffled groan.

"Thanks, mate. I'm in a bind."

As it turned out, Travis — the boy who helped in the kitchen — had called in sick and the girl that helped with the shopping and housekeeping had skipped town with her budding rock star/gas pumping boyfriend. This was a huge problem for Rog, who really couldn't get around the inn too well.

We were both irritable — he from the extra inn burdens, and me from being woken up too early. Cat Ass kept walking in and out of my legs, like he was trying to rub his stink on me and trip me up on purpose. He reeked. "Rog, this cat is obese — he can't even reach around to wash his own ass."

Rog's cheeks flared red. He didn't say a word as he wrote out my to-do list.

I was glad to get out of there and zip around in the Bug. First, I had to get some food and paper towels at the town grocer — *The Farm Emporium* – which is a weird name for a grocery store, if you ask me. When I got to the store, I was happy to find an open parking space up front. Just when I was about to pull in, another Volkswagen zoomed up and headed for the spot. It was a young kid driving the other Bug. He squealed to a stop. I waited for him to give me the bird when he stuck his hand out his window. Instead he waved me on, indicating I should take the space. Wow. Was it Volkswagen Bug camaraderie that moved him to such a generous offer? I pulled into the space, gave him a thumbs-up, and marveled at my luck. When I came to the entrance of the store, a young girl held the door open for me. No automatic doors?

"Do they pay you to hold these doors open, honey?"

She blushed and giggled, "Yup."

I scratched my head. "Really? Wouldn't it be cheaper to just install automatic doors?"

She giggled again. "I don't know." She reached for my shoulder and pulled a wayward thread off of my shirt. "Enjoy your shopping!"

Course, these days, Walmart has greeters, but it wasn't common in small towns back in the 90s. That 'hold the door for the customer' bit blew my mind. I roamed around produce and, mostly bored, I searched for the kiwis Rog wanted. A chesty redhead came over to me and offered to help search through them and squeeze for freshness. She stood there with her hands in her green apron pockets and awaited my answer.

All around me, store workers be-decked in green aprons stood at the ready. They were chatting amicably with each other and helping shoppers with their choices. I put the kiwis back. "No. Thank you very much, but, no...." I don't know why, really, but it made me uncomfortable. I was offered help in the cereal aisle, the foreign foods aisle and the soda aisle. The soda aisle??? Nice people — weird people.

I took Rog's mail to the post office and was escorted back to my Bug by the postmaster after I bought stamps. I took the Bug to get an oil change and was attended to by three grease monkeys who told me stories and made me *fresh* coffee while I waited. Anyone who's ever hung out at a garage while their car was being serviced knows they can never hope for anything better than coffee mud. We even played poker. I think they let me win.

When I got back to the inn, the place was buzzing with activity. The serious air from that morning had lifted and given way to giddiness. Other inn guests flitted around, all of them busy with something. They were fetching, eating, cleaning and asking Rog how they could be of service. That was a nifty little set up; 'come pay to stay at my inn and I'll put you to work.' Brilliant — very 'dude ranchy.' I cleaned up after Rog while he used his great culinary skills to prepare a scrumptious brunch. No one complained about the late meal. Cooking was cathartic for the big man — he was calm now and in his usual, jovial mood.

"Say, Casper, will you take a tray to Mrs. Franklin?" (Rog never called me by my real name — it was always 'boy' or 'Casper'.)

I swallowed a mouthful of ham. It was a tad overdone. "Yeah. She's the one you told me about when you told me that story about...."

"Ah, yeah, yeah," he cut me off like he was trying to get me to shut up. He gently pushed me into the pantry. "Hey, don't mention that shit around Mrs. Allen. She'll start thumping her Bible at us and I'm just barely keeping this blasted headache at bay...." He put boxes of cereal in my arms and pushed me back out of the pantry.

"What's wrong with Mrs. Franklin, anyway?" I dug in the box of Lucky Charms for the free leprechaun whistle. I didn't want that cardboard cereal, just the toy. I winked at

Mrs. Allen as she stalked past me with some spray starch. I think she growled at me. She needed a good smiting.

Rog didn't notice our exchange. "Mrs. Franklin is somewhat of a recluse. She's got a degenerative hip disease and it's just too hard for her to get around."

He had a faraway look in his eyes. For the first time, I realized Rog was sweet on her. He was an unimposing kind of guy, and I wondered if he had ever declared his amour outright. I knew he prepared food trays for Mrs. Franklin and sometimes sent his girl over to do some housekeeping. As it turned out, on that day, I was his girl.

I lifted the overly-burdened tray, which was loaded down with five kinds of meat. I went out the screen door at the back of the inn and started on the path that led from the Ox Blood, across the manicured lawn, and straight to Mrs. Franklin's house. The air was hot and sauna-like, which made breathing harder on this good ol' New England, late-summer morn. I was already sweating beneath my cuffs.

Mrs. Franklin's lawn was a field gone to seed. It was pretty in a wild sort of way, what with the wildflowers, and butterflies it attracted. Her house was old and not very well-kept, a white farmhouse that rambled on and on with a sloping roof that was barely propped over a concrete porch that had cracked and settled long ago.

I balanced my way up the disintegrating stairs and rapped smartly on a tinny storm door. I heard a shuffle inside and a thin voice that called "Come in." She had cleared her throat as if she hadn't spoken in a while and those two short words had caused her some effort. I walked through the front door and passed through what was probably a living room, seeing as how it contained a threadbare coach and an old Sanyo on a milk crate. There was a fireplace that had long ago belched out soot on the surrounding walls.

I rounded a corner and found Mrs. Franklin sitting at a deeply gouged and scarred kitchen table. There was a brown rickety chair and a questionable chrome chair as well, with a red vinyl seat. I chose the chrome and prayed it wouldn't give out underneath me. I set her tray on the table and folded my arms. That tiny thing — ain't no way in hell she ever ate a full meal that Rog sent over.

"And who are you?" Smoke poured from her nostrils, worked around her face and played over her withered skin. Her thin, brown hair was pulled back in a limp ponytail. Her eyes were yellowed and dull, but I could tell, intelligent.

"My name is Sebastian Park; I'm here to hunt your ghost."

When she smiled, the wrinkles left her mouth for a fraction of a second as her lips pulled up. She shifted in her seat and leaned forward to put a little more weight on the walker in front of her. The walker didn't roll — someone had removed the rollers and replaced them with sliced-open tennis balls. "Have you found anything yet?"

"No, and I need all the help I can get."

"Sure," she murmured. She sucked on her cigarette as if it were the very thing she needed to continue breathing. "People come to me all the time for help. I try my best."

Beyond the acrid smell of smoke, I got the whiff of something like boiling grass and old shoe leather. A big pot of something was steaming on the stove. I walked over. "Wotcha got here?" It was a clear, brown liquid with floaties.

"That's my home-made tea. I sell it in town and make enough money to buy food. The tourists really like my tea."

"Mmmm, yeah — doesn't smell like Earl Grey though, does it...."

She laughed. "That's medicinal tea, good for the nervous system, made from the best stuff in the forest." She shrugged. "Naturally, it smells a little earthy. That just means it's good for you!"

I think it was good for someone else. She wasn't looking at me just then, so I stuck my tongue out, gaggy-face style. I noticed she had a lot of photos on her fridge. I scanned a couple of them. "Who's this?" It was a ravishing blonde woman with Little Po Peep curls and startling blue eyes.

"Oh, that's my girl. Can't tell we're related, huh. She takes after her father's family." With one nicotine-stained fingernail she tapped the tabletop. "So what have you found out about our ghost? Come over here and tell me."

I sat down on the chrome chair, stretched my legs before me, and crossed my boots. I removed my Stetson, placed it on my lap, and ran my fingers through my hair. That's when I heard a tapping noise, coming towards me, down the hall. It was a black bird, walking across Mrs. Franklin's linoleum, with his claws clicking and his beady eyes staring. One of his wings didn't sit flat to his side like the other one did. "Whoa! What do we have here? Is that a raven?"

Mrs. Franklin chuckled. She took a little bit of something — a pellet of food, maybe? — from a cracked, plastic bowl on the table. "No, that's a crow — ravens are bigger. He broke his wing. I found him hopping around on my porch last year, waiting for me to invite him in and nurse him back to health. I can't set him back outside. His wing was broken, and now it's healed, but he can't fly. So, he would never survive out there."

As the crow passed me to get to Mrs. Franklin and his pellet treat, he looked at me sideways. I had a hard time maintaining my composure — if I had to pick between Cat Ass and that bird — I'd strap on a gas mask and cuddle Cat Ass to me evermore. I turned away from the bird and noticed a huge bag of cat food in the corner of the kitchen. "You got cats, Mrs. Franklin?"

She tossed the pellet down to the bird. He ate it, then clicked over to a piece of driftwood. He hopped onto the wood, then hop, hop, hopped sideways to its highest point. He flapped his wings a little and made small noises as he settled on the branch. Then he laid his eyes on me and watched. I shifted around and gave him my back.

"That cat food is for the raccoons — got a whole family of them that come to sup. You okay, Mr. Park? You have something on your mind?"

To my surprise, I found I was glad to have this moment with her, to be invited to talk about the awkward things I had been witnessing. "The people in this town are exceptionally friendly — but kind of nutty...." That sounded ungrateful. I winced at my non-customary lapse in performance. "What I mean to say is, everyone seems so happy, so willing to help, and so unprejudiced. The sky is always turquoise, except when it rains, because then, the sky cries drops of diamonds. The green is so green I can almost see things growing.

"Well, now you're just being silly."

"I admit, I'm theatrical. It's a wonderful town, but really, it's far from normal. And there's something else — I have never seen so many physically perfect people in one area in my life — you know? This is America, land of the free, home of the Belugas. But in Peachtree, the only overweight person I've seen is Rog." I slouched in my chair. That confession had taken the wind right out of me.

Her pastoral expression hadn't changed throughout. She just sat there like an animatronic smokestack. I sighed in relief, I didn't want to insult this woman whose house smelled like an eighty-year-old ashtray, and whose windows and drapes were thick with the yellow, sticky sludge of second-hand smoke. All of that didn't matter — I realized I admired her — a feeling I rarely felt for a woman. Lust — yes. Admiration — not often. There was no judgment in her eyes — she just sat there and listened to me. I liked that.

I thought of the things that contradicted my statement. She, herself, was a contradiction to what I'd just said. An example of imperfect health, what with her emaciated body and smoking vice. There was Roger — who couldn't keep himself from a tray of brownies even if there was a knife at his throat. There was my friend at the diner who did things to me against the oak tree that would get her drawn and quartered by any number of feminist groups. There was Rog's housekeeper who'd just run off with her boyfriend, leaving his mother bereft. I had heard her sobs through the phone when she called the inn, searching for her son. So, not all was perfect in Peachtree. "Hey, even though everything in Peachtree isn't quite perfect, it still seems far from normal. Something feels off — what is it?"

She smiled. Everyone smiled in this town. You could ask them, 'Gee, where is the funeral home?' and they were certain to smile before they answered.

"This is a town of good people. It is a town that draws good people — repels those that are not so good."

In my mind flashed two unbidden memories. The first was about that moment when I arrived at the town hall and stepped from my car — that feeling of shame. The

70

second, was later on, when I left the town hall and watched the families in the park. Both moments felt very wrong — like I didn't belong, and I should get out of Peachtree as soon as possible. It was more than discombobulated nerves. It was a persistent feeling that I was still trying to suppress. I really wanted to leave, but I really wanted to get paid even more, so the nagging feeling was something I fought down every morning for breakfast. "I've been having funny feelings — like there's someone watching me." I cleared my throat. "...and I'm not a guy who's prone to paranoia."

She started to laugh. She laughed so hard she lapsed into a spasm, and choked on her smoke.

It made me uneasy to watch her struggle like that. For her, it would be a race to the finish line — complications from her failing hip or death by inhalation.

She was finally able to take a breath. "Well, then, you've got some skeletons in your closet, haven't you." She ground her cigarette in the ashtray. There were at least twenty other butts in there.

I pictured a hundred — a thousand — naked women in my proverbial closet. They were quiet, but their faces were sad and angry and pleading. I closed the door with meek apology.

"Don't worry about it. The people who live in this town are good people. We laugh, we cry, we have petty arguments here and there. But we have no violence, no crime greater than Harley Bobkins getting drunk on payday and streaking down Main Street. And so what — what's a flailing penis among friends?"

She shocked me on so many levels, I was momentarily speechless. "Fascinating." I put my elbows on the table and rested my chin in my cupped hands.

"Yes, it is, and there's no place else like it on Earth. We've actually had some bad types come into town, reeking of violence. They never last more than twelve hours. They just seem to drift away of their own accord. Personally, I think the good in this town is so strong, it drives them off. They don't care — they have the rest of the world to pillage and plunder." She lit another cigarette.

I shifted and must have appeared extremely uncomfortable, because the next thing I knew, she was trying to console me.

She leaned forward with effort and took my hand. "Oh, I see now why you're squirming over there. No, I'm not talking about your kind of bad. I mean people much worse than you." She rubbed her hand back and forth on my hand, then moved herself into another position — some weight on the edge of her chair, some weight hunched over the walker.

"Do you think there is a person behind your ghost? Rigging some wire and lighting — smoke and mirrors — that sort of thing?"

"Oh, I don't know, Mr. Park..."

"Sebastian..."

"...Sebastian. I really couldn't say. I've never seen it myself, but then again, I don't get out much."

I frowned as I chewed on my bottom lip. She moved around in her chair and looked out the window at the mountain across the way. There had been mist there at its base early this morning, but it was now mostly dissipated.

"Can't anyone point me in a direction? Anyone?" Peachtree was a small town. I assumed they all talked to each other. She didn't say anything for a while. Lift, suck, expel. Lift, suck, expel. I wrongly assumed she was trying to protect someone when I pressed again. "It's okay — I'll treat them with respect.... If someone around here knows who's responsible for your ghost, just point me in the right direction and I'll ferret them out with charm."

Not a word.

My cranium wavered like a bobble-head. "Anyone?"

Her lips moved behind the yellow haze. "When I need to know something, I go to the trees. Go to the trees, Sebastian."

"Go to the trees and what?"

"Go to the trees and ask them for answers."

My elbow slipped off the table. I had to catch myself and sit up straight. "Oh — ask the trees — okay...." You should have seen me try to keep a straight face after that. I left soon after. When I got to her front door, I was surprised to see a strange, round man on her stoop. He was wearing a sports jacket with threadbare cuffs that was ten times too small for him. E.T., the Extra-Terrestrial, was on his old, faded t-shirt. I pulled the door open and greeted him.

He gave me a lopsided grin, pushed past me, almost knocked me into a dusty cabinet containing a strange little curio collection — also dusty.

"Okay, then, have a good day...." But the weird dude probably hadn't heard me — he was already out of the room and gabbing away in the kitchen.

Chapter 6

I trotted back to the inn. I found Rog in the backyard, applying white paint to several strips of molding that were stretched over two sawhorses. I scratched my head. "Your neighbor..."

"Pamela...." He put his brush down on the cover of the paint can, then motioned for me to follow him into the house. He wiped his hands on his work pants as we made our way into the pantry. He started taking Mason jars of peaches down from the top shelf and handing them to me.

"...yeah — Pamela — wants me to go into the woods and ask the trees about the ghost." I tilted my head as I gave him the, 'she's-a-fruitcake-right?' look.

His laughter was a friendly growl. "So, what are you going to do?"

We took the jars to the kitchen counter and opened a few. "I don't know. I'll go, I guess. I like the woods. At the very least, I'll get to take in some of your beautiful Vermont wilderness...." I clapped my hands together. "Yes, I'll go! Pack me a pic-a-nic basket!"

He grinned. "Yeah, at the first hoot of an owl, don't worry — I'll have your bed all clean and made up for you, back here."

"Hey, hey, hey! You underestimate me! I camp out in New Mexico all the time!"

Rog squinted at me. "In your head, is camping synonymous with homelessness?"

I sniffed. "To each his own." I got a silver fork out of a drawer, pilfered a jar of peaches, and headed upstairs to plan my expedition. I was almost to the top step when I plopped a peach in my mouth and gagged — that jar of peaches had gone south. They tasted like the smell of vomit. I spit the offending thing back in the jar and wiped my chin on the back of my sleeve.

That night, I had a dream. A dream about dancing chickens. They were animated, but not alive — not in the traditional sense. They were on a gaudy, turn-of-the-century vaudeville stage. Naked chicken carcasses doing the Cancan. I was the only one sitting in the theatre, on the threadbare, red velvet seats, and I was starving. The dancing chickens turned me on. I left my seat. As I walked up the aisle, my shoes stuck to the tacky floor. I got on the stage, on my belly, and rested my head on my folded arms. I loved how the chickens swung their pimple-skinned thighs around and around. I got up on all fours and crawled to the closest one, the one at the end of the line. They seemed oblivious to my advance and continued to Cancan to some rowdy music that sounded like it came from a scratchy phonograph player behind the decrepit stage curtain. I reached out and snatched the chicken on the end of the line and brought her cold, firm thigh to my lips. The others kept dancing. She kept moving too, in time to the beat, like she was an Energizer chicken that wouldn't stop. I gnoshed on her leg, biting down over and over, with my eyes closed, in complete ecstasy. When I opened my eyes, I started screaming — it wasn't a chicken thigh in my hands, it was a woman's thigh, and there were gouges taken out of it and teeth marks everywhere.

I heard whimpering. The theater seats were now filled with women — all kinds of women — and they were crying. They were all missing one leg.

I woke up screaming. And hungry.

By morning, the dream was a hazy memory and its horrific hold on me had significantly weakened. I showered and headed to the town hall to appeal to the mayor for an advance. He was in a meeting, of course — I could hear the Ping-Pong ball being paddled back and forth — and I was left to squirm on the Puritanical bench and ogle his sexy, old assistant. She was firm and curvaceous in her knit dress, and — wily me — I had to close my mouth to keep from drooling. She must have gotten take-out too, because the office was filled with the scent of jasmine chicken or some other fragrant Thai-flower food. Lotus beef? Orchid duck? Who knows.

"How's the hunt going, sweet thing?" She pinched my cheek as she walked by. Her charm bracelet rang as she lowered her hand.

I shrugged. "Every time I think I've got a direction to go in, everything changes. I've branched out and am applying wacky methods to track this thing down. I don't know what I'll do when I find it — but at least I'll be able to give ya'll a better idea of what it is. And, like they always say, 'once you know the monster, you can conquer the monster."

"Well, I certainly hope you're right. I was bowled over by that thing once. Did I ever tell you? Made me puke black bilge for a week...."

I frowned. "No kidding?"

She sat down next to me. I was definitely going to stop at the Thai place for lunch. "No, I'm not kidding. At first I thought I had gotten food poisoning — *Ma's Breakfast* holds onto their ham steaks for too long...and I really should have known better — but anyway, I ate black licorice that day, too, so I thought I was puking up that.... But no, the licorice eating and my run-in with that thing were on the same day — and you don't puke up black licorice for a week."

"Jesus, what happened?"

"You mean when I encountered it?"

I took her hand and nodded.

"I don't know, it was months ago. I was working in the garden. It was pretty early, I hadn't had breakfast yet and the garden was soaked with dew. I wanted to get the weeds out while the ground was soft. At first I was enjoying myself, and then all at once, I felt like I wasn't alone. I turned around and there was this black cloud, right there behind me. And it was like it was conscious and waiting for me to notice it, because as soon as I turned around and gasped, the thing leapt at me! It coated me, and I swear on the Bible, that thing tried to get in my mouth! I didn't scream. I kept my lips clamped tight and since I was hunkered down anyway, I tucked my head between my knees. Don't know why it worked, but when I brought my head back up, the thing was gone. Only, I felt awful and queasy, like someone had forced me to eat a pan full of old, congealed grease. That whole week, I thought I was sick with food poisoning. Then I thought maybe I was sick with fright.

83

But now, after talking to others who had almost the same experience, I think that thing made me physically ill." She gave an unhappy chuckle. "You know how you can convince yourself that what you're suffering is anything other than what you're afraid of...."

I bumped my shoulder into her shoulder. "That's terrible. I'm so sorry."

"Yes, well, you just help us get rid of that thing, Mister."

My meeting with the mayor was uneventful. He was on the phone with someone else the entire time. He kept nodding at me when I spoke and waved a Ping-Pong paddle at me in a threatening manner. I didn't think he listened to a word I said until I got up to leave and he snapped, "You can get your camping gear, Mr. Park, but it will be coming out of your pay...." Fair enough. I mentally added another two weeks to my hunt.

I was on my way out of the office when the mayor's assistant called after me. "Oh, Mr. Park, I was wondering if you wanted to take a look at this book here — it's a history of Peachtree. It might help and it might not — but you know what they say, 'history repeats itself.' Maybe you'll get inspired."

I needed to appear like I could still be their top gun, so I took the book this time, and with profuse thanks. "Thank you, my girl. Now, point me in the direction of that Thai restaurant because your take-out smells absolutely incredible."

She tweaked my nose. "I don't have any take-out, silly; and I wouldn't have Thai — I'm allergic to curry *and* cumin — have you ever heard of such a thing?" Her trilling laugh was light and airy.

I didn't feel light and airy. No take-out? Then what in hell was that smell? A lump formed in my throat. *She* smelled like that smell. I didn't ask anything else. I said

85

goodbye to her, then walked slowly down the granite stairs, back to my Bug. I threw the Peachtree history book in the back seat and quickly forgot about it.

I drove to L.L.Bean in Freeport, Maine, and bought hiking boots, cargo shorts, a Swiss Army Knife, a tent, sleeping bag, mess kit, camp grill, a plethora of questionable magazines....

When I got back to town, I fished in the glove box for the town map the mayor had given me at our first meeting. I decided to hike around Peachtree's outskirts and crisscross its middle. I needed the strenuous exercise to exorcise the shit that was going on in my head. The camp fire at night, my magazines – they all worked to sedate me — it was pure bliss. On the second day, I got bored of the hiking and decided to hang out by a shallow section of the river.

I had picked up a hiker's folding chair at L.L.Bean, and a lantern. I set my chair before the river, anticipating a lazy afternoon. I sat down, crossed my new hiking boots at the ankle, and cleared my throat. At my feet, the river ran slow. In the shadow of a rock, a big fish lay still in the water. The only time it moved was when a hapless water bug jittered across the surface of the water and the fish flung its body up and caught the bug in one wide-mouth swallow.

I was embarrassed, but I actually tried to talk to the trees. "Hello, trees, I am the great Sebastian Park, ghost hunter to the stars. I will now converse with you." Maybe they found the rich baritone of my voice overwhelming, maybe they were sleeping, or maybe they were snobs. At any rate, they didn't answer me.

I went back to town to complain to Mrs. Franklin. She was at her kitchen table — I wondered if she slept there. Her ugly bird was on the tabletop and she was stroking its head. I noticed the drift wood was leaning against the table; I presumed that's how the thing gained access to the surface where she tried to offer me food. When I whined that the trees wouldn't talk to me, Mrs. Franklin choked on her smoke as she laughed.

"Sebastian Park — you have to eat, sleep and *live* the trees if you expect them to talk to you. Listen to me. Leave your fancy trappings behind so you can go get your answers." She pointed to the doorway that led to the room right off the kitchen. "Go to my bookshelf and get my field guide. It's the dog-eared one."

I went into the next room and reached for the most ragged book I could find. It was covered in half an inch of greasy dust. I wiped it off on my cargo shorts and went back to her table. I held the book out to her.

"No, Mr. Park. You keep it; that book is yours now. Use it. You'll get your answers. And you'll need to leave it all behind — the equipment, the food, those magazines...."

I raised my eyebrows. "The magazines, too? You must be kidding!"

"Yes, those magazines.... Just your sleeping bag, matches and a pan." She flicked her hand at me. "Off you go."

Chapter 7

I returned to the same spot by the river. It took about twenty-seven hours for the green around me to start looking like something I'd want to eat. Up until that point, I'd been boiling my river water, drinking my dandelion tea, and grumbling over my idiotic choice. "Why am I doing this?" I yelled at the setting sun, then stayed there and kept doing it. I ate cattails and wild asparagus and made continuous sour faces while I munched. I avoided plants with spines and plants with milky or discolored sap like the guide said. I felt dizzy from hunger and exhausted from lack of Whoppers. I stopped thinking about how it was that I was whiling my days away in the middle of nowhere, Vermont. I began to believe Mrs. Franklin — there was something in the air here, an invisible tent that enclosed the town.

My libido dulled. I was by no means a eunuch — I checked — but I had no cravings. I slumped in my chair and ran my fingers through my hair. The heat wave wouldn't let up. I could smell the rocks baking by the river, and as the temperature climbed, so did the shrieking pitch of the cicadas. Time passed. I meditated. Really, I 'vegetated' but I'll say meditated because that sounds acceptable and excusable. Soon it was dusk. The pinks and reds of sunset turned to black and the wind picked up.

By then, I was very dizzy. I assumed I had eaten something that was toxic, because my vertigo had mounted and every breath I took could hardly get down my swollen throat. When I closed my eyes, the symptoms got worse. My eyeballs were stabbed with bright flashes of neon color. I forced them open and there before me was a black cloud of I-don't-know-what over the river. Screaming, I jumped up from my chair and toppled the lantern onto the rocks of the riverbank. I looked down at the lantern debris then up again, and of course, there was no black cloud there. But there were other spots — tiny black spots that danced over my line of sight and in the corners of my peripheral vision. Crazy old woman and her field guide — I was obviously drugged on some woodsy shit and just starting a long, hellacious trip. I kicked the debris out of my general living area and took the kindling that I'd gathered earlier to a sheltered spot between two boulders. It took several attempts to get the fire going. My eyeballs vibrated in their sockets as I watched the flames build. There was a noise coming from the woods, a whispering. The sound was barely discernable, but I could actually make out a voice and some words.

Go now

I didn't breathe. I scrunched my eyes shut, though they strained to pop wide. A voice of alarm screamed in my head and drowned the chorus of whispers — that, and my pants caught on fire, which sent me screaming to the river. The frigid water extinguished the flames and the cold sliced into my shin — where I was sure third-degree burns were getting ready to bubble up. I stood there for a long while, letting the river take the heat from my leg. The queasiness was so bad at that point, I started to dry-heave as I stood bent over the black water. And this is the crazy part — all I could think was that, if only I had Peach Dumpling's cheeks to suck on, I'd feel better. I didn't want her over the hood of my car, I didn't want her sucking me dry — I just wanted to smell her cheeks and nibble on her skin. I was famished. I squatted down in the river and felt around under the rocks not really knowing what I was searching for.

Under the light of the rising moon, I sloshed out of the river and headed downstream. The further I went, the more the river widened and became shallower. I ended up in the marsh of cattails where I had dined earlier. It was quiet there, and still. I got on my hands and knees and moved slowly, straining to see in the dark. I dipped my shoulder down so the moonlight could pass and light the water in front of me. I moved slower and deeper into the small marsh. I lifted my hand out of the muck and was about to put it down again when I noticed a bullfrog, still as stone, staring at me. I halted. As slow as I possibly could, I leaned towards him. I took an entire minute to move my body forward. I got as close as I possibly could before I suddenly leapt at him, like a pouncing cat, and grabbed him with both hands. He felt wonderful, squirming in my grasp. His wet, silken skin glided over his soft struggling bones. I pushed his slim belly across my lips as I sat on my haunches, not caring that my ass was soaked. I held him up, over my head and

94

dangled one of his legs in my mouth like it was spaghetti. With quick reflex, he drew the leg up and croaked in protest. I couldn't wait anymore. I mashed his belly against my face, felt his skin cover my mouth, and bit into him. He was chewy and tender all at the same time, and as his fluids dripped down my chin, I could smell the earthy river-smell of him. I licked the open wound a few times.

An owl cried. Out of the corner of my eye I saw his shadow come at me and felt the wind from his flight as he swooped right over my head. This broke the spell. I screamed as frog entrails and saliva tumbled out of my mouth. Sputtering and swearing, I spat out the cold frog flesh and tripped out of the marsh.

The fire was still lit when I got to camp. I swiped at my mouth while I gathered more kindling and bigger branches. I huddled around the fire till dawn. I refused to listen to the trees that whispered to me and I prayed for the neon lights and the black spots to leave my eyes.

At dawn, I ran out of the woods and jumped into my car. I raced to Mrs. Pamela Franklin's house. I burst through the front door and rounded the two corners. I knew she would be sitting at that table, smoking. I threw myself on the chrome chair, slapped my palms on the table and leaned towards her noxious fumes. "I heard them," I hissed.

She poked out the cigarette. "What did they say?"

"They said, 'go now.' It freaked me out!"

The peaceful expression she always wore left her face. Trees talked to me! "Why did they say that?"

She shrugged. "I wish I knew."

Then my emotions went sour. A queer sensation tightened my belly, not unlike the wrenching in your gut the morning after a bender My elation at having heard trees speak vanished as I finally homed in on the realization that I had murdered Kermit last night — that I had actually put him in my mouth while he was still moving. I shifted uneasily in my seat as Mrs. Franklin shifted uncomfortably in hers. The crow came tapping into the room. He squawked and made me jump. Sheesh! I looked away from him, desperate to look *anywhere* else. I feigned great interest in a box of stale doughnuts on the chipped Formica counter — which probably tasted like smoke — a blackened toaster, a family of ceramic bears that could hold flour, sugar, whatever. "I'm a fraud." I jumped again, as if the voice came from behind me, though it was true enough that I said the words myself.

"Well, of course you are, but you're here now, and you're a strong, young man. I suspect you're capable of actual work to obtain the honey pot that's coming your way?" She lit up again and stared at me with a raised eyebrow.

"Yeah, but, it's just this…there's something I'm not telling you…. And I don't think you could handle it — I did something last night that I'm not incredibly proud of…."

"Mr. Park, I was a war nurse during Vietnam. I once helped to surgically remove a suffocated rodent from a lonely soldier's anus. That boy sent me Christmas cards till '79,

when he fellated his pistol and blew his brains all over the

Thanksgiving turkey. Now, what would you like to share

with me?"

I stared at her like your average mouth-breather.

"Okay, I don't know if this tops that, but last night I hunted

down a bullfrog and shoved it in my mouth while it kicked its

little legs and tried to escape." I shook my head and

murmured, "...grossest thing...."

"Now, now, Mr. Park — no need to insult an entire

race — frogs are a very popular food in Asia — and

sometimes while they're still alive. Maybe we shouldn't

make you go into the forest *au natural*. Maybe next time you

should pack some light food for yourself." She was suddenly

very intense. "And maybe next time you should take a friend

with you, someone to keep an eye on you. I heard you've

gotten to know that Angel girl at the diner...."

Who the hell told her that? "Why the hell would I want to go back in the forest?"

"The trees are talking to you, Mr. Park. You must have some latent talents that are just emerging. You should be thrilled. Maybe you'll hear them talking to you again. One thing is for sure; we've been seeing this black ghost in town for over a year now and nobody knows more about it today than they did back then. Use your talent to find out how to get rid of it. Go meditate or have a séance or whatever it is you people do, and bring us some news."

"So far, the only stories I have of this black fog is from people who have seen it when they were alone. Has this thing ever traipsed around a crowd?"

"Well, sure, at *The Farm Emporium*. Several times."

"The *grocery* store? Now why the hell would it go there?"

She lit a cigarette. "People have seen it move clear across the parking lot."

I put my head in my hands. "God love ya — this is a wacky town. Why didn't you say so in the first place?"

"Well, I thought you had tried there already. I know Rog sent you just the other day...."

"He sent me for kiwis; he didn't say anything about the ghost fog."

She shrugged. "Been plenty of sightings over there."

We sat quietly for a while. I stopped drumming my fingers on the tabletop. "Oh, what the hell — come on, Pamela — we're going on a stake-out at the grocery store."

It took a while for her to get to the Bug, but we managed with time and a few wry jokes. We got a bucket of chicken at *Rhode Island Red's,* Peachtree's source of fried chicken, then we Bugged on over to *The Farm Emporium.*

Townsfolk came up to the Bug. They leaned on the hood and hung out while Mrs. Franklin puffed away. Randomly, I craned my neck around the party in the parking lot to keep myself on the job. The whole scene reminded me of the nut-job crowds that wait on desert hills for UFOs. I hoped somebody would go by with a vending cart — I wanted a pair of antennae.

The good people had a lot of questions. When they asked about my progress, I told them that I had, with my equipment, discovered the ghost was deriving its energy from the grocery store's generator and when it came for a refill, I was going to nab it. This excited the crowd and left many of them in a happy mood of positive action.

Inwardly, I was grim. It still bothered me, those two words that the trees said. *Go now.* Who was supposed to *go now*? Was it a threat? Was I supposed to be doing something more than sitting in this parking lot and guiding Pamela on long, slow, bathroom visits?

"Why do we have to get rid of this black thing anyway? Has it ever done anything to anyone?"

"It's a negative energy; it makes people sick Mr. Park— hasn't anyone told you that?"

"Yeah, well, a couple of people have mentioned getting sick. Rog told me it made him sick. But his peaches made me blow chunks and no one called in the exorcist for them.... Shit!" I accidently knocked the box of fried chicken off my legs. The 'Meat Man Platter' tumbled all over the gear shift and slimed it up. "Aw, man! I have to clean this up. I'm going in to the store to buy wipes. Be right back."

I hoisted myself from the car and stretched out. I waved to two giggling girls who bounced by in short skirts and halter-tops. Lord, have mercy! I followed them into the store, thankful for a change in scenery and rubbing at my still-hungry, growling stomach. The girls laughed harder. They must've thought I was growling at them.

I roamed through produce searching for a snack. I sniffed the grapes and grimaced — everything smelled like crap these days.

Jasmine Hawk rear-ended me with her mother's cart. Her mother was at the deli and hadn't even noticed six-year-old Jasmine had wandered across the aisle to pay a visit. "Hi. I like grapes. My mom bought some for me." She threw her long hair over one shoulder, dramatically, as if this was a big-girl action she had recently acquired and was trying out in public for the first time.

"You're so right, Jasmine. Grapes rock."

"This is my dog, Gipper," she held out a limp stuffed animal and prattled on, "I want to take him for walks but I have to carry him because he's not real, but my teacher is going to be Miss Crabtree this year, you made some grapes fall down."

Her mother was in a ham and cheese ordering oblivion and still failed to notice Jasmine's escape. I picked up the grapes.

Jasmine had more to say. "If I stop wetting my bed then I can have Barbie sheets."

"That's great, Jasmine. Maybe you should go back with your mommy, over there, she might be worried when she turns around and sees that you're not there."

"Nah, I told her I was coming over to see you."

"Ah." I prayed to the fluorescent lights and found no help for myself up there.

"I don't pee in the bed because I'm scared."

"Oh no, I'm sure."

"No, it's just because I can't wake up, see that guy over there?"

I saw who she was pointing at. It was the weird round-dude I had not-quite met on Mrs. Franklin's stoop. He stood hunched over in the foreign foods corner, talking to himself. He was wearing the same E.T. t-shirt and the same sports coat. Suddenly, he jerked his head. When he saw me he started to whisper to himself. One of his eyes was roving off-center. He let a container of sprouts slide from his hands, then disappeared around the corner. I frowned.

"Yeah, he's like, you know, he's like rain, I'm going on a Disney cruise in eight weeks! I hope it doesn't rain then!" Her eyes glittered; she searched me for signs of mutual excitement.

I was feeling a little tripped up, a little peculiar — as if I had just touched something slimy, like yesterday when I went to put my sneaker on only to discover Rog's cat had puked in it. I felt the sudden need to rush. I took Jasmine by the hand and walked her to her mother sans carriage. Jasmine was still talking. I pointed out the carriage to Mommy, and raced to the Bug.

"Pamela, I just saw someone in there, he gave me the creeps. Jasmine Hawk said, 'He's like rain'."

Mrs. Franklin narrowed her eyes behind her smoke. "Ah, don't children love to speak in riddles."

"Yeah, you gotta admit, he's one weird dude — he bumped me into your curio cabinet when I left your house that first day we met."

Mrs. Franklin chortled. She stared at the potted plant display outside the front of the store. "That's just the mayor's boy, Al. Others call him 'Allie,' but I think they're being condescending, so I just call him Al."

"Yeah, well, he gives me the heebie-jeebies." I gunned the engine of the Bug. "And I'm tired of waiting for some cosmic tailpipe to fart out your ghost, Pamela. I'm taking you home." When we passed the diner, I blurted, "I'm going back out to the woods. I don't know why, but I can't get it out of my head — what the trees said to me. I have to go out there."

She nodded. "Do what you need to do."

When we pulled into Pamela's driveway there was a red Camry parked there.

I shut off the ignition. "Who's that?"

Her eyes shined bright as a little girl's. "Oh, that's my friend, Patricia — she's come to visit me!"

"Didn't she know you were on an incredibly long and boring stake-out at the Emporium? Everybody else did."

"Oh, we girlfriends have a sixth sense about things."

She moved as fast as she could towards the house, pushing her walker hard. I could see little spasms of pain affected her by the way she cringed and groaned. When we went into the kitchen, the place was cleaned up and smelled fantastic. The table was set for two with cloth napkins and matching silverware, and there was a pot of meatballs and sauce simmering on the stove. The women hugged over Pamela's walker. I checked out Patricia as Pamela introduced us. She was wearing a skirt and jacket suit, pressed, with a white, ruffled shirt. Her hair was pinned up high, like a Gibson Girl. She stood erect as a corseted school teacher from yesteryear, and wore bright red lipstick.

I extended my hand. "Very nice to meet you, Patricia."

He hand was thin and cool. "The pleasure is all mine. How are you finding Peachtree, Mr. Park?" She reached down to pick up and cuddle that blasted crow. It was odd, the way she crooned to that bird. If I was wearing such a pristine suit, I wouldn't want that thing rubbing against me. Okay, I wouldn't pick that thing up and cuddle it no matter what I was wearing. It just sat there, cozy against her bosom — giving me the dirtiest black-beady-eyes.

"Well, I know where the grocery store is...."

She had a warbling laugh. "Ah, ha! You've learned so much about our lovely town already!"

"Have we met before?" Yes, this is an old line, but really, I had seen this woman somewhere before.

Pamela and Patricia exchanged looks. Patricia answered. "I work at the welcome center out on I-89. Did you stop there on your way in?"

I knocked on the table. "That's where it was! You gave me pamphlets on Ben and Jerry's and the Cabot cheese place. Didn't you tell me there was great hiking out here, off Old Crabapple Road — or was that Putney?"

She warbled again. "My, you have a great memory for faces, Mr. Park!"

"Only when I'm stunned, Patricia — only when I'm stunned." I pulled a chair out for her so she could sit down, then I served them both dinner. "Ladies, I must go. I have pressing business and lots to do to prepare for it." I kissed Pamela's dry, bony hand. "Madame, thank you for the delightful stake-out." I kissed Patricia's hand. "Madame, thank you for the cheese info. I bid you both adieu!" I bowed.

They clapped as I left.

Chapter 8

"But why won't you go?"

I was at Angel's apartment, whining in the bathtub. She had an apartment over an ice cream shop. It was much more comfortable than the tree at the diner. Angel was strolling around the apartment in Wonder Woman underwear, sorting laundry to different drawers. "It's just camping, Angel. I want to spend some time with you."

"Then rent a room at the Ritz-Carlton in Boston." Her voice was flat. She didn't say anything else while she shook the wrinkles out of a tablecloth.

"Angel, this is Vermont, an outdoorsman's paradise. Let's go frolic in nature. Besides, I can't leave — I'm on a job. And part of my job right now is going into the woods." I pouted. "And I don't want to go alone. Come with me. Please? Pleasepleaseplease?"

She smirked, sauntered over to the tub, knelt down, and rested her breasts on the porcelain edge. "Why? What are you going to do to me out there?"

I eyed her glorious epicenter. "We'll start with whatever hasn't been done to you yet...."

She squealed. "Fine, but one night only — and I don't think I'll be able to make it through that. She whipped a huge sponge at my chest and laughed.

In the morning she cooked me some bacon and eggs — a veritable vixen she may have been, but a chef she was not — then we headed out to a different part of the river than the place where I had my bullfrog nightmare. By noon, we were actually having a great time fishing in the river, baking in the sun, and telling lewd jokes. She wore her Spiderman underwear, fishing waders and sun block. I wore my red boxers, fishing waders, and a tie around my head — don't ask — the past couple of hours had been very gymnastical. We fornicated and slept all afternoon, then added more wood to the smoldering coals of our fire. Earlier, before we drove out to the trailhead, we had picked up all kinds of meat, prepared foods, fruits and vegetables at *The Farm Emporium*. When we sat down to eat, I had a few hot dogs and steak tips, mainly because the pasta salad was yellow and the roasted vegetables just seemed kind of bland — like I was eating grass. We took a long walk after dinner, but made sure we were back to camp by twilight so we could set up for the night. The tent had to be repositioned a couple of times because there were rocks everywhere and we had to blow up the air mattress manually — the pump was shot — but otherwise, we had a pleasant evening and were all ready to go at it like rabbits.

"Baby, come here, feel this." She was sprawled on a large boulder; belly down, wearing nothing but electricity.

I took off my sweaty shirt and rubbed my belly. "What is it, darlin'? You need help over there?"

"It's this rock, it's incredible. It soaked up the sun all day long and now it's warm, warm, warm." She mewled like a kitten and rubbed her cheek on the stone's smooth surface.

I dropped a pan that I was going to wash in the river, ran into the tent, and got the oil. Then I hopped out of the tent, caught my foot on the fly and ripped the whole thing down in less than a second. I flicked the tent off my boot like it was toilet paper and got to Angel's rock just as soon as I was free.

I'll always remember that moment, running up to her, anticipating her as she lay stretched on that boulder. It was a lover's night — clear skies and the intoxicating scent of wild plants as they cooled off in the night air. The sound of the river had put us in a trance and washed away every worry. If I could have stopped that moment, I would have. I would have existed with that one woman forever, with the stars never extinguishing and the fragrant dark holding us.

I quickly got my pants off, jumped on the boulder, and clambered over to her. I straddled her rump and held the bottle high as I spilled oil on her back. She sighed. I smeared the oil all over her back and her ass with both hands, then began to knead the muscles in her neck.

Something stank. One time, after another hiking trip with an avid rock climber, I forgot to get the beef jerky out of my pack. When I got home, I threw the pack in a seldom-used corner of my closet, swearing I'd never woo a rock-climber again. I don't know why I was with her anyway — heights freak me out. Over time, the stink in my apartment increased. After a couple of months, the new love of my life

(I forgot her name) asked me if I had any mouse traps in the house, because my place smelled like moldering rat. Instead of having fun, she insisted we search for the dead rodent. It didn't take long to find the moldy jerky in the closet in the bottom of my bag. Heinous smell — and that's what it had started to smell like in the woods. It was taking over the scent of wildflowers and fecund earth, and even over-powering the clean smell of rivers and rocks. But this magnificent girl was writhing beneath my thighs, so I dismissed the smell and concentrated on her smooth, tight skin.

I began to salivate.

I pressed my fingers into her spine and kept the pressure on as I drew them all the way down to her tailbone. I pressed my thumbs into her ass cheeks and pushed as I ground my teeth. I backed up and bent down, pressing my lips to her oil-shined buttocks. The world grew hazy as my eyes rolled back and I opened my jaw wide. The next thing I know, I heard a loud voice in my head yell, "NO!" Suddenly, Angel was screaming and kicking me in the head. There was blood all over her rear end, her legs and her back.

"What the fuck are you doing, you goddamned prick?" She got up on her knees and cried as she looked back at the bloody bite mark on her ass.

There was blood all over the rock and down my chest. I slapped my hand to my mouth and stared at her without blinking. I didn't know what to say. Had I really done that to her? I didn't remember doing that to her.

She shoved me so hard I fell off the boulder. "Take me home, right now, you psycho."

I watched her stomp to the tent. The smell of rancid rot grew stronger. I saw movement out of the corner of my eye. A tall thing came out of the woods not twenty feet away. The smell of vinegar and foot fungus grew stronger as the creature limped forward. It looked at me as I sat there cowering. It looked at Angel and stared as she tried to force the zipper open on the crumpled tent. She didn't see it. The thing was tall — over eight feet — and stood hunched like it was too weak to hold itself up. There was a hole where a nose should've been, and when the wind blew its long, scraggly hair, I saw an ear was missing on that side of its head. The thing's body was emaciated; every bone was outlined under the thin, peeling skin. It advanced on Angel. I opened my mouth to scream, but no sound came. In my head, I heard the voice of the trees say a loud, clear sentence.

You must leave now — run!

The next few moments seemed to happen in slow motion. It walked up behind her, reached for her head and grabbed a fistful of hair. As she screamed my name and reached up, it wound her hair around its fist. It took hold of her sweet chin and twisted her head in one quick motion, causing her neck to make a loud snapping sound.

I sat huddled like Gollum as I watched it eat her. I hated myself for the erection that wouldn't go away and the hunger pangs that urged me to join it in consuming her. I used the boulder to drag myself to my feet, then took off into the woods — a naked, snot-nosed, sniveling-mess, that was covered in a dead girl's blood. I must have gone more than two miles when I suddenly heard a howl, a shrieking wail that rang through the woods and made me crash into a tree. I got up. In a daze, I started limp-running in a different direction. I didn't know where I was. I didn't know how to get out of the woods. I just ran and ran, till my deep breaths burned my chest and throat. I ran right into the thing, bounced off it as it screamed in my face, and showered me with a blast of air full of phlegm and chunks of flesh. Its putrid stink made my eyes water. I twirled around and went careening in a new direction. It gimped up behind me and drove its claws into my back when it shoved me. I fell down, tasted dirt and felt it grab me round my midriff. It shook me and shook me until everything turned black.

When I woke up, I was laying on the forest floor. Birds were singing and the sun was warm on my face. Every muscle in my body felt like it had been massaged with a cheese grater, and I had no feeling in my right hand. My jaw was stiff. When I opened my mouth, a deep cut on my bottom lip opened up and blood poured out. I was freezing cold and incredibly filthy, covered in congealed blood, dirt and dried sweat. Something smelled real bad — something meat-based — like it was infested and crawling with maggots. When a little breeze came, it blew the smell away. But when the air was still again, the stink intensified and made me gag. I lay there for a while, gagging, and wondering what in the world had happened last night. When I thought about what had happened to Angel, I covered my face with my grubby hands and cried. What was I going to do? If I went to the cops, I would never get a fair trial — 'Bigfoot' ate my girlfriend — wasn't going to get me out of this. I was covered in her blood. And that nightmare thing wasn't Bigfoot — I didn't know what it was — but it wasn't Bigfoot.

I knew what I had to do, and I really couldn't face it — I had to go back to that camp. I wished I didn't know how to get to camp, but I had a pretty good clue as to how to go about it. Not ten yards off, the river sang across the stones. To my right, broken branches and blood, blood everywhere showed me the direction I had come from the night before. This was the way I had to return.

Next to me, at the base of a wide pine, there was a mound of fresh dirt. It looked like a burial mound. My throat was dry, so it was hard to swallow. I crawled over to the dirt pile, disgusted with myself for doing what I was about to do, because I knew what had to be under that fresh dirt — the putrid smell had intensified as I got closer to it. I pawed the dirt away like an old dog until I exposed slimy bones that were covered in ants, a mass of ants so large, I could hear them crawling over each other and over the bones. They made a small tk-tk-tking sound as they worked at their meal. I cried out and slapped the dirt back over the bones; the whole sight became a blur as my vision focused and unfocused. A little ways over to my left, I saw another burial mound, and another.

It took me several minutes to get to my feet. I had twisted my ankle the night before, when I bounced off the tree, and now it was blown up into a full cankle. Most likely it was sprained. I went to the river and kind of crumpled into a sit. I sat crossed-legged, cupped my hands, and brought the freezing water to my face. I cried. I had watched a woman die last night. I sat there as she was being murdered and I had watched. A woman I had made love to. A woman I was fond of. I gagged and spit into the river. I hated my disgusting, worthless self. While the sun forced its way through the pines and dappled the river, while the chipmunks bitched at each other in the trees, and while the blue jays bullied smaller birds, I cried. I sat there till my skin shriveled up and my fingernail beds turned blue. The day was wearing on, I had to get to that campsite.

I found a stick to serve as a crutch and followed the river. I'm glad no one came across me, a naked mess with blood-crusted hair — I would've frightened the shit out of them.

Before I arrived at the campsite, I smelled the still smoldering fire. I came around a cluster of thick bushes and stopped. Where the camp should have been, it wasn't. Everything but the fire was gone. No tent or supplies. No blood on the rock. No body. I clung to the walking stick and scanned the woods to see if the person who had taken all the stuff was still around. A human had done this, most definitely. But who? And why? Was that thing just a person in a costume? I don't know why I even thought that question — that thing from last night was not human. The way it moved like an animal — it was nothing a human could ever fake. So was there a person working with it? I brought my hand to my mouth and stared. Who would possibly work with such a creature? Did the monster even have the intelligence to communicate with a person? How did it control its eating habits? It *ate* human flesh.... Then I remembered — it didn't eat me. For whatever reason, it had chased me down and taunted me and then left me there in the forest — alive.

I hiked out to the trailhead, still naked. I found a t-shirt in the bug, one sock, and a pair of Angel's superhero underwear — Batgirl with ruffles on the ass. I put the t-shirt on, threw the sock into the car and sobbed while I put the Batgirl underwear on. When I got to the inn, Rog barely moved his eyes from his crossword puzzle as I limped up the stairs. I heard him chuckle behind me and make a comment about what a winner I was.

In the shower, I stared at the wall, while I scrubbed the blood from my body. In a daze, I shuffled to my little room, lay on the bed, and stared at the ceiling. Paranoia walked all over my chest. What the hell was going on, and who was involved? I couldn't trust anybody. And why had they called me in? Was I really supposed to stop a black fog? Or was I supposed to stop a murderer straight out of the Cryptozoology books? And why had they called *me*? This was way, way, way out of my range of expertise. I had no expertise. Were Angel's bones in the fresh burial mound? Would anyone be looking for her? People knew she went camping with me — what was I going to say when the inevitable questions were asked? Guilt, shame, and stress pressed on me like a bag of cement.

And I was hungry. I wanted meat. I wanted to eat Angel. That's when it hit me — whatever that thing was, it had infected me. It was the reason I craved human flesh.

Chapter 9

Rog Haversham, owner of the Ox Blood Inn, didn't think a man should stay in bed all day. It was near 7 p.m., and that sissy-haired Casper boy hadn't come out of his room since he had taken a shower, hours earlier. Rog liked the man okay, but boy, oh boy, did that New Mexican have peculiar ways. He suspected Casper was under the weather — Ghost Boy didn't seem his usual strappin' self when he went limping up the stairs earlier. So, Rog decided to do what he did best — cure the lad with food. He breathed heavily as he ambled up the stairs with a tray of newly-simmered chicken broth, saltines, and ginger ale that he had shaken until all of the bubbles were gone. The good-for-nothing Travis boy followed him with a box full of Casper's stuff that they had found in his Bug. Rog clomped down his narrow hallway until he reached Casper's door. He yelled, "Got some grub for you, boy, and some stuff from your car in case you need it." But Casper didn't answer. With a meaty fist, Roger fished out a set of keys from his no-iron Dickies. Wouldn't be the first time someone committed suicide in an inn. And although he didn't really think Casper offed himself, the lad *had* come into the inn wearing ladies underwear and scowling about something. Maybe he was gender-confused; *that* caused a lot of chaps to off themselves. He sighed as he let himself in the room. Sebastian was lying on top of the covers and snoring. Rog huffed out a sigh of relief and with a multitude of hand motions communicated to the good-for-nothing Travis boy to put the box down and get out. Rog put the tray on the little table by the side of the bed, then leaned over Sebastian. He held his hand to the cowboy's head — the lad had a fever. Rog sighed again and went downstairs for Tylenol. When he got to the landing he found a new couple had arrived at the inn and wanted to be shown around the place. During the kafuffle, he forgot about his patient.

***

I wasn't sleeping when Rog came in. All that man wanted to do was talk, and I couldn't handle that right now. And why the hell was he touching my forehead — to see if I was dead yet? I got up and ignored the tray of broth. Tequila, man! Bring me tequila when I'm sick! I felt woozy, like my head was trying to take off and swim around in a bowl of warm Jello. I squatted over the box of stuff from my car — town map, one sock, girly mag, ghost hunting books (props), and the Peachtree history book which was jauntily entitled *Peachtree: A History.*

Read it.

I cried out. What was that? Who just said that? The trees followed me into my room? Cold fingers played down my back. Someone was in the room with me. I gasped and fell on the hardwood floor. Holy shit, after all these years of faking it, I — Sebastian Park — was experiencing a real ghost. It was amazing, and scary as all hell. The room had grown colder, the air tasted like electricity, every hair stood up straight on my neck and my skin tightened uncomfortably. *Peachtree – A History* started vibrating. Honest to God, that book started dancing across the floor towards me. I crab-walked backwards yelling, "Hey, hey now — you stop that!" All at once, the book did stop. It just sat there at my feet and didn't move anymore. I picked it up and put it in my lap. I opened it spoke to the empty room. "Okay? Is this what you want?" Warm air flooded the room, the electricity left, my skin calmed down and I was left with an empty feeling. I got up and limped to bed with the book. Rog came up an hour later, smelling like boiled hotdogs.

I pointed to the book. "It says in this book that Peachtree is proud of its Native American roots. Really? I haven't seen any sign of that around town, I mean, no shops, no signs, no fundraisers...no indication of Native American pride whatsoever."

He felt my forehead with his big beefy hand. "You've got a fever, you damn fool. Why didn't you come down and get some medicine?"

"Really, do you even *have* any Native Americans living in this town?" I hit his hand away from me.

"What's gotten into you? And what the hell is this?" He moved the hair at the side of my neck. "You got dried blood over here — why the hell do you have dried blood on the side of your neck?"

"Git yer hands offa me! You got any NAs living here or not? I need to talk to someone...."

"Holy hell, Casper, what are you on about?"

"Yeah, and you got ghosts in here, too. I just had an episode with one not an hour ago...."

He sat on the bed beside me and almost made the mattress flip. "My great-gram was Abnaki...."

"Yeah, but are there any Native American groups in town, a council — you know — somewhere I can go to talk to someone...."

He raised his eyebrows. "What the hell for?"

I clamped my mouth closed. There were a million and one thoughts slamming around in my head and I needed to keep them all to myself. Maybe I couldn't trust him — how would I know? "Listen, I need to look busy on this case — everyone knows you consult the Native Americans when you got a nature spirit roaming about, like ya'll got."

He sniffed. "Everyone knows that, huh?" He scratched his chin. "Nope, no councils here. There's a sizable council two towns over, but that's all I can think of.

Pamela's got quite a bit of Indian blood, you wanna go talk to her?"

Peachtree: A History vibrated in my hands. It made my bowels clench up and strain. "Ah, no — let's not talk about this to anyone just yet. Not till I get my story straight and sound feasible."

He blustered. "You know, Casper, plenty of folks are scared about this black fog that you haven't seen yet. I hope you don't get attacked by it like I was, I hope you don't get sick like I did — like many of us did. But, I also hope you start taking this seriously or just move yourself out of town...."

I felt suitably ashamed. "Aw, buddy, I believe in your black entity. And I want to help, too. I need more time, though. I need to do more research. I know I act flippant, but I'm really trying to help here."

Rog hung his head like a little kid. "Yeah, I believe you're a good person under all that prettified shit you put out. I've always believed you'd do the right thing. I've always believed you'd be the one to help us — I'm a bit psychic myself." He looked around the room. "I can even tell you had a female ghost with you in this room, not long ago. Now, I'm not good at this, but I'm getting a name. Does 'Sophie' mean anything to you?"

I swallowed. I wanted him out, and quick, before I lost it altogether. I swallowed again. "No."

Rog shrugged. He laughed. "Guess I'll have to keep practicing." He got up. "I'll go downstairs and get your Tylenol and I'll write out directions so you can go visit your Native Americans." He shook his head and left the room.

I was suddenly bathed in sweat. Sophie was my grandmother. Shit. Had that been her all along? When I first heard the whispering in the woods and thought it was the trees saying, "Get out," was that really her? The voice I heard today, in my room, was the same voice I had been hearing all along. Not only that, the voice came with a feeling — just like in a dream when you're in a strange house and it doesn't look familiar but you know it's yours. You can feel it. Was it my grandmother that day on the granite stairs at the town hall? The more I thought about it, the more I felt like she was the one who was making me feel uncomfortable. Like she had been trying to push me out of town. Could it really be old Sophie? Rog didn't know me and he certainly didn't know my grandmother was named Sophie. I could tell by his face when he asked if I knew anyone by that name — he was completely oblivious. So had my grandmother Sophie been trying to get me to leave this town from day one? Why? What did she know that I didn't know? And was I not a complete, sorry faker like I thought I was? Did I have some of her psychic gift? I sat up a little straighter in bed. Pride filled me and warmed my chest.

I stood up and swayed as the room started to spin round and round. I guessed it really was a pretty good fever. I winced and moaned as I pulled on a clean pair of jeans, alpaca socks, and my shiny never-been-bled-on, ostrich boots. My L.L.Bean hiking boots were gone with the tent and the supplies, even the cooler full of food. Cleanly removed. *Who did that?* I looked at the small pile of clothes — Angel's underwear and my old t-shirt — as they lay in a corner of the room, crudified with blood and dirt, and soaked with rank sweat. Destroyed. When would people start asking about Angel? Why hadn't anyone called the inn yet, searching for me because they were searching for her? What was I going to say? Certainly not the truth. I went to the closet and shook a button-down shirt out of a dry-cleaning bag. I put the shirt on, buttoned it up, and stared at the pile of clothes in the corner. I sighed, picked up the underwear and the t-shirt, put them in the dry cleaning bag, then crumpled the whole mess up and tossed it on my bed. I used the toe of my boot to scatter the dirt that was left behind on the pristine wood floor.

I gimped downstairs and there was Rog, at the last step, holding the Tylenol out to me. "I have a question." When I made no move to open the Tylenol bottle, Rog took it from me, opened it up, and tipped out some gel caps.

"Here, shut up a minute, and swallow these first." He held out a glass of cranberry juice.

"I keep seeing this strange guy. I first saw him when he charged into Pamela's house one day, and then I saw him at the grocery store. And when I saw him at the grocery store, I swear, he got spooked to see me and he took off. He's a round little guy with a roving eye, wears a sports coat even though it's been like living in a jungle around here. I don't think he's all that old, and he has a way about him that sticks in my craw. Mrs. Franklin told me it was the mayor's son."

Rog looked at me like I was being silly. "And?"

I raised my eyes heavenward. "I don't know; something isn't right about that guy."

"Of course something isn't right about that boy. Follow me." We walked into the dining room. He took me firmly by the shoulders and sat me down. "I'm going to get you a cold cloth. You really need to get back to bed." He tsk-tsked and pushed through a swinging door into the kitchen. When he came back, he held a soggy dish towel and was yelling, "Where do you think the oatmeal goes?" Then he grumbled something about 'dumbass kids' and, 'Jessica wasn't nearly as stupid.'

Travis followed Rog out of the kitchen carrying a tray of sausage, cheese and crackers. Travis seemed hugely bored and didn't seem bothered by the fact that everything on the tray was about to slide off and go crashing to the ground. Somehow, he made it to the table without accident. He hung his head as he walked sullenly back to the kitchen, almost dragging his knuckles. I winced at the sausage. Blek, it was cooked. Then I realized what I had just thought, and I felt like crying. Rog saw my reaction and thankfully mistook its meaning.

"No appetite, huh? Well, of course not — you're as sick as a dog. Sip your cranberry juice and take it easy."

I winked my horror away. "Thanks to you, Rog, I'll neatly skirt any oncoming urinary tract infections, too. Cheers."

He sat down with a whump.

I suddenly smelled ass; that damn cat probably decided to pass out under the table.

Rog reached for the food tray. "Now, why are you asking about Allie?"

"I don't know — I just have a feeling." I think my cheeks turned red. "I've never put much faith in the 'I have a feeling bit,' but I've been having lots of feelings lately..."

Rog was looking at me funny. I realized I was rubbing my chest like I was experiencing a mild heart attack.

"...and believe me, I've learned my lesson — the hard way — that it's best that I investigate these feelings when I have them."

He patted me on the back like he was a proud father. "Oh, my boy ...all grown up." Then he actually wiped a tear from his eye. It was all a little bit awkward.

"So what about Allie — why do you want to know about him?"

"When I was at the grocery store, I was talking to that little girl, Jasmine..."

Rog harrumphed, "Cripes, man! And you escaped?"

"And she said something cryptic about Allie. She told me, 'he's like rain,' and just when she said that, I got the weirdest feeling — it made me feel a little weak." I shrugged.

His face softened. "Now, now, boy — that's a good thing. You should go with a gut feeling. You should trust it. Though, why you had such a feeling about an addled boy like Allie, I don't know. He's never caused any trouble around here — just acts weird is all, and that's on account of being dropped on his head as a baby."

I snorted. "You're kidding, right?"

Rog held up his hand — three fingers pointing straight up and his thumb holding down his pinky — Scout's honor!" Then he couldn't suppress a barking laugh when he said, "Mrs. Mayor used to put her baby boy in the laundry basket, on top of the dirty laundry. He used to scream like the dickens if he wasn't with her, so she invented all kinds of ways to take him with her and get the housework done at the same time. All of that must have made her tired, as you can imagine. Now, I don't know how tired you'd have to be to drop your kid in the wash, but that's exactly what she did. She picked up dirty laundry basket #901 and shook the load into the drum of her top-loading washing machine. She didn't know what she had done till she heard crying beneath her unmentionables." He moved his bulk around on his seat and must have kicked Cat Ass because I heard a little mew of complaint from under the table. "Next thing you know, boy doesn't cry much anymore after that, and he's had a big ol' dent in his head ever since."

I stared at him. "Oh, give me a break...."

He shook his head. "I'm serious! That's a true story — go ask him yourself. He likes to talk about it. Most days you can find him on the job. He works at the cemetery; he's the caretaker...." All this time, Rog had been pawing at the crackers and cheese and he was making a huge crumby mess.

Outside, the sun had already set, and through the inky darkness, I could barely see the shadow of the apple tree. Was I going to go out there now, to the cemetery, to interview a brain-damaged man, the night after I watched a monster murder my special lady friend? Fuck no — I might be slightly stupid, but I'm not B-movie stupid.

Under the table, Cat Ass let out an S.B.D.

I groaned. "I'll head over there in the morning."

"Whatever suits your fancy. I'll write up those directions I promised you and pack you a lunch. I think you've got a long day ahead of you."

Painfully, I got to my feet and limped a couple of steps away. "You're a good man, Rog." And he was a good man, a great man. I was sorry I had made fun of Cat Ass.

He indicated my bum leg and frowned. "You just stay out of trouble, ya hear?" He got up and started to clear the dregs off the table.

Chapter 10

"Well, good morning Mr. Park. Would you like to come over for a spell before you start your day?"

It was just after 6 a.m. — what was Mrs. Franklin doing? She was already set up with her chair and table and freak-bird in a play per. "Up early today, aren't you, Mrs. Franklin?" I didn't have time for her hootenanny.

"Not at all. Sometimes I can't sleep whatsoever — pain in my hip and such. That lovely Roger set me up early so I could get some sun on my face while he tends to the needs of you all and that inn."

"Truly, he's a wonderful man." I was walking to the Bug as I spoke so she could see that I didn't have time to stop and talk.

"Oh, Mr. Park...."

Geez. She was straining her voice trying to get my attention. I put the directions Rog had written for me and the cooler that contained my lunch on the passenger seat, then trotted over to Mrs. Franklin's side. That nasty crow cawed at me from the play pen, then fixed his eyes on me the entire time I tried to make nice with Mrs. Franklin and get the hell out. I looked at the inn and saw Cat Ass standing on a chair, his front paws on the window, his wide belly almost filling the glass. He moved his mouth like he was crying. He tilted his head and cried again. It was strange, Cat Ass wasn't usually vocal. Too bad he wasn't stealthy enough to go out and eat that ugly crow.

"Where are you off to in such a hurry?" She pointed to an empty lawn chair beside her.

"No, honestly, I can't, Pamela. I have so many errands to run today."

"Oh, too bad." She bowed her head as she twisted her fingers in her lap. "I know it's only been days, but I feel like I haven't talked to you in forever. Any news?"

Images of Angel being eaten and memories of running scared through the forest overtook me and made me weak. "Can't say that I have anything right now, but let me go and I'm sure I'll come up with something today."

She looked shocked that I was evading her. I felt so guilty. Why couldn't I just stay with her for five minutes and give her some stories? But I couldn't. I felt compelled to get going. I mentally added 'gung ho' to the list of new emotions in my life. I shrugged and thumbed the Ox Blood Inn, "Do you want me to get him for you?"

"No. I don't need Rog." She was staring down at her bird and didn't say goodbye to me when I left.

***

Peachtree cemetery was a grand affair, hilly and ornate, with lots of black, wrought iron gates. It was creepy as all get out. It was almost 7 a.m. by the time I arrived. The sun was up, but the cemetery was dark. The old gnarled oaks were huge. Their leafy arms reached out till they touched one another and cast the place in perpetual shadow. I parked the Bug down front, by one of the three entry gates. The middle entry gate was wide open. The gates that flanked the middle entrance were locked up tight and topped with long, pointy spires to ward off those that would climb over. The well-worn footpath that led around the end of the fancy stone and iron fence was a much easier way to access the cemetery when the gates were locked.

I walked through the wet grass, up the hill towards an especially large mausoleum that sat in the only patch of sunlight. The grass, because it was protected from the scorching sun by the leaves above, was the richest shade of emerald green. On the tombstones that surrounded me, weeping angels rested their heads on folded arms. I'm sure they were beautiful when they were carved, and as inspiring as their creator must have meant them to be — but now, many of them were covered in lichen and moss and sporting broken limbs. On some, mold had filled their eyes, making the sockets black and empty-looking. Many of the stones had fallen over, or had been tipped over, and lay cracked and broken. At the base of several stones waved little American flags, drooping flower arrangement, or fake flowers drained of color by countless rainstorms. The deeper I walked into the cemetery, the more uneasy I felt. On the road below, a car passed by. A little girl had her mouth pressed against the

146

window in the back seat. I wished I was in the back seat of a car with my mouth on a window and going away.

I skirted a thin, ancient stone. Its epitaph read:

> Christian stand still and pray a bit
> here lies the farmer Gauthier
> He had to pay too dearly for his sin:
> He died of self-brewed beer.

I mumbled, "God love ya, buddy," and took a deep breath. All this walking uphill was quickly wearing me down after my evening of bloody terror, two nights prior.

When I reached the mausoleum, I leaned on it to catch my breath and hold my face up to the beautiful sunshine. My ankle and knee on the same leg were screaming in pain. I should've gone to the emergency room, but they would've asked questions and I wasn't able to answer the simplest question at that point. It was like this — if I opened my mouth to speak one word of what happened that night, even one fabricated sentence to explain my whereabouts, I would have broken down like a crazed man into a drooling, raving rant. A rant I never would have come out of. So, I kept my mouth shut and my mind on the mission.

A murder of crows flew into the tree right next to me, cackling and cawing like witches. Behind me, at the very back of the cemetery, was a big barn made of corrugated metal. I walked towards it on the cemetery road which turned from pavement to dirt as I got closer to the building. There was a Kubota tractor parked outside — a backhoe, with a bucket on one end and a digger on the other. This must be what they used to dig the graves. No hand-shoveling to the bottom like the old days. Next to the tractor was a white pickup truck. I peeked in the bed of the vehicle. There was a mountain bike in there and a bunch of dirt and debris.

The barn had a garage door entrance, which was locked, and a regular door entrance which was closed, but opened easily when I tried the handle. I jumped. I wasn't expecting that door to open. It meant I'd have to check it out. I shut the door and stepped back from it. I didn't want to go inside that barn. What was wrong? I was used to skulking in cemeteries — it was my job as a ghost hunter, after all. But I was the most frightened I had ever been in a cemetery as I stood outside that barn door. I stepped forward, reached for the handle, and walked in.

I found an oddball collection of things in there — suitcases, bicycles, chairs, and boxes filled with knickknacks. There was a black Camaro covered in dust with a little dashboard Chihuahua. An Armani suit still in a dry-cleaning bag hung on a hat tree next to a pair of fire log tongs. Dolls, ride on toys, and baby carriages. Grimy bottles of tequila, old cans of beer and liquor everywhere. There was a U-haul trailer with a flat tire. A barrel full of rowboat oars and fishing poles. Three rows of coolers piled five high. And clothes — clothes in every nook and cranny. Why was all of this here? Was it stolen?

"That's my stuff, mister...."

I yelped and jumped a foot into the air. I whipped around to face the short, cock-eyed man who stood in the doorway. Yes, I saw the dent on one side of his head now. I could also see by the lock on his face that he wasn't angry at finding me inside his barn. He wasn't afraid, confused, or suspicious — he wasn't displaying any of the normal emotions an enraged, guilty man should display. His jaw was ajar and his good eye was far off in Dreamland. I forced a deep breath into my lungs and willed myself to unclench my fists and calm down.

"It's great stuff — just great!" I walked towards him as my skin shrink-wrapped around my bones. I offered my hand. "Great to meet you, I'm Sebastian Park. You're just the man I was hoping to meet." Sweat rolled into my eye.

He frowned at me. "I'm not supposed to talk to you."

I backed up a step, into a kayak. "Oh, yeah? Who told you that?"

The frown melted and suddenly there were tears in his eyes. He shifted his weight from one foot to the other. "My daddy told me not to talk to you."

My grimace hurt my cheeks. "Don't worry, buddy, I won't tell him!"

He bobbed up and down on the balls of his feet and giggled. He could change expressions like a cartoon flip book. "You won't?"

I shook my head hard.

"Okay, then!" His smile was big and toothy — clearly not faked — as he started in on some verbal diarrhea. "Yes! This here is my stuff! It's the best stuff in the world that my father lets me keep out here but tells me not use so it won't break I pick it up around town so it doesn't stay out there all trashy do you want to see some of it but you can't touch it cuz it's not yours you see...."

Oh, Christ — I didn't want to walk into that mess with him as my guide. The open door and bright summer sunlight seemed so far away from me. I pressed my lips together. "I'd love to go check out your stuff with you."

He barreled past me and began to explain, at length, the color, size, and make-up of each thing he pointed out. He told me the name of each thing. He told me the use of each thing. It was getting hot in there — the metal walls and August sun together made a nice big oven — and I started to get dull-witted from the heat and dust.

"You probably know what these are...." His goofy cheeks were red as I walked around him to see what he was rambling about.

My balls pulled up inside me.

He was pointing at a backpack — Angel's backpack. There was a mess of clothes pouring out of it. At the top of the spew sat a pair of her superhero underwear. I gasped, but he didn't seem to notice. He went on and on about how it wasn't nice to play with lady's panties. I leaned against the Camaro and said in a raspy voice, "How did you get all this?"

He beamed. "I'm the one assigned to clean up the town. I do a good job."

"How did you get that backpack?" I wanted to kick him in the head, but something held me back as I clenched my teeth.

"That's from a campsite I had to clean up — woo-wee! — what a bunch of messy pants *they* were!"

'Messy pants?' That's what he called us? Suddenly, the heat, the dust, Angel's pack, and his behavior were all too much. If I didn't get out of there fast, I was going to puke all over the Camaro. I ran for the door, tripping over I don't know what. I heard him yell for me to come back and see his marble collection.

As I careened down the cemetery road, the weeping angels watched me in silence.

Chapter 11

My drive away from the cemetery was a blur. Why was this happening? Why had I been called here? These people had a legitimate, humongous problem. Why didn't they call a legitimate, hugely popular psychic celebrity? They could have news coverage on this black smoke. Why me? I was beginning to realize why — that guy back there, Cemetery Boy, had no idea what he had in his barn, but I bet my roving one-eyed-snake that the mayor sure as hell did. I should leave this town, get the hell out quick. If the mayor was in on...whatever...and he was the one who hired me...something real bad was going on. Would his dim-witted kid tell him I had seen all the treasures in the barn? Should I go to the cemetery to bribe the kid into being quiet? I wasn't going back there to talk to good 'ol Al — no way.

I wiped the sweat from my eyes and hyperventilated all the way to *Ma's Diner*. I had to go there — I had another bad feeling.

It was high-breakfast time and the place was busy. There were a couple of stools available at the counter, so I took the one closest to the pastry display. A sallow, middle-aged woman with bad breath offered me coffee.

"Sure, I'll take coffee." I didn't drink it. I searched for Angel, knowing Angel wouldn't appear. I waited for someone to ask me about her, and no one did. No one had called Rog's place asking for her yesterday or this morning. Should I ask about her? I swallowed the bile in my throat as the sallow woman came to check on me.

"Can I get you anything else?" She eyed my unsipped coffee and frowned.

"Where's Angel?" I blurted then rubbed at my bugged out eyes.

The woman 'pffft.' "That girl? Who knows — she's totally unreliable." And that was it — the waitress walked off.

I knew I was gawking. I knew I wasn't blinking, but couldn't help it. Wasn't anyone searching for Angel? I pushed off the counter and bashed some broad in the shoulder as I tottered for the exit. I got into the Bug, slammed the door, and stared out the window. I stayed there for a long time. Why? Maybe I was waiting for the cops to come and take me away. Nah, I knew they weren't coming for me.

I reached over and picked up the directions that Rog had written out, the directions to the Indian Reservation two towns over. It was the same town where that sassy girl worked, at the convenience store, *The Black Chicken.* I drove over there and was happy to see her working inside — unjustifiably happy. I felt like Angel's death was entirely my fault, and in my silly misery, was comforted by the fact that I hadn't caused this girl in *The Black Chicken* to come to any harm.

I didn't go in to see her. I revved the Bug and drove to the Res. It was gated. The gate was secured with a padlock, and there was a big sign that read: Closed To Visitors. I heard an unmuffled or poorly muffled car roar up behind me. Whoever it was tooted at me to get me out of the way. I backed my Bug up so they could pull in my spot. A lanky teenager with long dark hair got out of his little Japanese car and unlocked the gate. He gave me a once-over that clearly said, 'You stay there,' then got back his car, drove through, got out, and relocked the gate. All the while, he kept a wary eye on me.

Dejected, I drove to the center of town, parked in front of the town hall, and watched a homeless person feed pigeons in the park across the street. A homeless person — now that was more like it. I had been relaxing by degrees ever since I left Peachtree. This horrifically dirty, homely, homeless person made me want to jump for joy. This town was already more normal than Peachtree. I worked up all the nerve I had and entered the town hall. I roamed around the multiple halls of the hushed building and poked my head into all of the rooms.

I had a plan to get on the Res. It wasn't a very good plan, but what the hell was a good plan under these circumstances?

Then, I struck gold. I walked in on an open town meeting and sat in the back of the room. There were two other spectators besides myself. Three tables had been pushed together in a 'U' shape, and the town's political heads sat bored and fidgeting around the structure while one of

158

them droned on about the possibility of town sewer. Next, they fleshed out the possibility of Mr. Thomas McMurphy building on what may or may not be protected wetlands. Then it was onto Akins vs. McKinstry and who was at fault for Akins unleashed dogs eating McKinstry's uncooped ducks. That's where I fell asleep. I woke up when the energy changed in the room. They were all getting ready to leave. I jumped to my feet and kicked the folding chair in front of me by mistake. I lunged for it, fumbled, then shoved it into place with a clank. "Wait, wait!" I yelled and all heads turned towards me. "I have an issue, or rather, I have to take a movement...or whatever...put it this way, I have something to ask...or put before you..." I rubbed the ache in the back of my neck. "You know what I mean, right?"

An library-type lady dropped her attaché case to the table with a bang. "Well, get on with it — what is it?"

"Great! Thanks." I cleared my throat and put all my weight on one leg. I folded my arms across my chest. "The lovely people of Peachtree hired me to rid them of a...paranormal phenomenon that they have been having trouble with. It's been several weeks, and I haven't been able to...finish my job. I have reason to believe that I need Native American expertise on this and couldn't find anyone suitable that could help me in Peachtree. I'd like to gain access to the Native American Indian Reservation here in your town."

All eyes were on me, and all eyebrows were raised.

Library Lady said, "You're kidding, right?" She picked up her attaché case. "And we can't grant you access to any Indian Res — that's their business."

I shook my lion-maned head, which was frizzier than ever — what with the summer heat and intense stress. "I'm sorry, ma'am. In fact, I am not kidding. And truly, I need help here...."

They had all been still for an entire two minutes, right from when I made my first outburst. Now they started to talk in low murmurs and continued on with their packing up.

One by one, they walked by me and left the room without making eye contact. Finally, only Library Lady was left, the unlucky recipient of my question. She walked right up to me.

"Psssst...."

I pulled my head back, why in hell had Library Lady just 'pssst' in my face?

She pointed towards the front of the room, to a man who sat in the second row. "There's your guy, gorgeous. He comes to every town meeting to make sure we don't fuck up. To the back of the man's head, she said, "G'night, Buck."

The man raised his hand to indicate he had heard her, but he didn't turn around.

She brought her attention to me. "Good luck." After checking her watch, she left the room.

I scrutinized the guy. He had a long salt-and-pepper braid, silver rings on the fingers that gripped the chair in front of him, a silver cuff bracelet with a *huge* turquoise stone, and leather coat — suede — that was trimmed with

161

feathers and leather fringe. I walked to his row, sidestepped towards him between the chairs and sat down two seats away from him. "Hi, sorry if I sound crazy, but I'm running out of options." I held out my hand. "I'm Sebastian Park."

He accepted my proffered greeting. His handshake was warm and strong as he squinted at me. "You're in a shitload of trouble, son."

Chapter 12

I gave him a ride to the Res. I didn't ask if he had a car or where it was. My head was spinning with what he had said. Actually, my head was spinning at his tone, at the conviction in his voice when he said it — he wasn't fooling around. We rode in silence for a short while. Then, with all the grace I could muster, I stuck my foot in it. "Thank you, for having me on the Res — this means a lot to me and I really appreciate you having me. Believe me."

He waved his hand at me. "It's nothing and stop calling it a Res. It's just land that a bunch of us co-own, which makes it private land, and hence, the fence and locked gate."

I was flabbergasted. "Really?" We who were born and raised out west assumed there were Reservations everywhere, because out west, there are.

"Yes, really. Most of us were forced out of Vermont in the 1600s. You wanna find my cousins, you wanna go to the Reservations in Canada — that's where most of them ended up. Those that stayed in Vermont married white folk so they wouldn't get shot. There are a lot of us still in Vermont, but we tend not to congregate lest we get thrown in jail again. The seven full-blood Abenaki families living on my land are a bunch of racy hooligans, marrying our own kind and living in privacy and all. As long as we don't produce any two-headed children, they leave us alone."

I glanced at him sidelong to see if he was kidding.

All he said was, "Mind if I smoke?"

"Be my guest."

He pulled out a pipe, filled it, and puffed it to life. Then he turned towards me and expelled a lungful of smoke straight at my face. 'Awkward' doesn't adequately describe this moment — the Bug is a small vehicle and we were two big guys. Not only was he leaning into my personal space, but he was in my space blowing smoke at me. I turned away from him and blinked a couple of times. Then I turned back to question him but was at a loss for words. He was just sitting there, quietly puffing away as if nothing had happened.

He pointed a long, crooked finger. "Pull over here."

He had me pull off to the side of the road, kind of in a ditch, so he could unlock the big cattle gate and let it open. He swung his arm around and around like a flagger starting a drag race to get me to pull through. After he re-locked the gate, he jogged over to the Bug and got in. He was surely a spry old thing.

"Okay, now you wanna pay attention to the road because it takes sudden turns and it's dark out here."

I nodded. "Okay...WHOA!!!" I slammed on the brakes just before we hit an old junk- heap of a Cadillac. Apparently the road made a ninety degree turn right there.

He sniffed. "Told ya so."

I cranked my wheel to the left and proceeded at a miserably slow speed. After another ninety degree turn, again, for no apparent reason, the Bug's headlights highlighted a double-wide. The yard out front was strewn with bicycles, cars, and a little shed with a sign on it that read, 'Sue's Jewelry Shop.'

"Keep going; I'm further up on the left." His pipe clicked against his teeth.

I pulled into his driveway, and there was another double-wide. It was cute and clean with flower boxes at the windows. On the ground were raised garden beds lining both sides of the long driveway. In them, were shrubs I couldn't identify.

"Roses," Buck grunted and waved his hand, indicating I should hurry up and get to the house already. "Come on in and meet my woman."

I followed him into his home and was met by a blast of air that smelled like the best chicken pot pie in the world. I sighed. I didn't want it. I should have been hungry, but I didn't want chicken pot pie.

We stood in the kitchen while a small woman quick-stepped down the hall. "Another stray, Buck?" She didn't smile as she pointed to a seat at the kitchen table. She wasn't being unfriendly when she didn't smile; she just seemed like a woman who was all business, with a brisk, no-nonsense attitude. Buck sat too, as she started putting out place settings, five in all, which meant someone had not yet arrived. The plates didn't match, but they were all French toile decorated with pastoral scenes. The pot holders that hung by the stove were macramé art and the pot on the stove was huge and dented.

"Our friend here, is named Sebastian. Sebastian visits us from Peachtree, though he is not originally from Peachtree...."

Mrs. Buck had been in the middle of stirring in the great big pot when she stopped mid-stir. She turned around. The worry lines on her forehead deepened. "I'll get the sage — but we're having dinner first, Mister. I didn't sweat over this chicken pot pie in the August heat for nothing." She crossed her arms over her chest and stared me down.

Buck got up, held her, and kissed her on the head. "Of course you didn't, Cooing-Dove, and I'm ever so appreciative for this meal. Don't worry. It'll be all right."

She smacked him in the ass. "I'll give you, 'Cooing-Dove.' She kept glaring at me over Buck's shoulder while he continued to hold her.

I squirmed in my seat.

Buck moved his braid over his shoulder and winked at me as he sat down. "That's her given name, but we all call her Dove."

"Nice to meet you, Dove."

"Nice to meet you, Sebastian." She gave me her back and resumed stirring.

The entry door opened and a young couple came in. The young man seemed surprised to see me, but he was still laughing about something the girl had told him. "Whoa," he chuckled, "who brought pale-face for dinner?"

He was the same young man who was not-so-hospitable at the gate earlier. Now, as he held out the chair for his girl and turned and straddled his own chair, he seemed relaxed and cheerful. He reached across the table to shake my hand. "What's up, buddy?"

I shrugged. "Too much, unfortunately." I couldn't take my eyes off of his girl.

Dove snorted as she brought the pot pie to the table and everyone clapped. "You can say that again."

But I hardly paid attention to what Dove said. The young girl had skin the color of dark honey. Her eyes were wide and dark and fringed with long lashes. She had an incredible shape, I could see beneath her thin form-hugging sleeveless top and snug jeans, all curves and no jelly. Full lips....

My mouth began to water.

"Sebastian, here, hails from Peachtree — only he's not originally from Peachtree and he's come here specifically to seek help."

The young man swung his head around to gawk at me. "Ooooooh...."

The young girl spoke, her voice was warm and quiet, "Dude! Are you for real?"

Dove had served them all and now she sat down. She brought the first bite of food to her lips and said, "Yes, dude — very real."

The girl let her eyes roll over me and I let my eyes roll over her. I bet her thin fingers tasted like salt and honey.

She said, "Something's not right about him."

Buck swallowed a big forkful of mashed potatoes. "We know."

The girl leaned over and pulled at the chin of the young man until his attention was only on her. "Do you mind if I test him? I mean, really, what are the chances of this happening in our lifetimes?"

I was wrong — there was some good meat on her. Her breasts were full — plump, plump, plump. I pushed the pot pie around on the plate.

Dove looked at the girl and snapped, "Savannah, this is not a game, you know."

Savannah held her hands out in a placating manner. "I know, Mother-in-law, I know. But he should be tested…it's the only way we'll know for sure…I mean, I guess we could call in a reader…but why wait?" She took the young man's hands. "John, what do you think?"

He kissed her on the nose. "I think you're a wild woman, that's what I think." He hugged her to him, knocking his fork off the table. "But I also think it's dangerous — what if he actually bites you? I mean, shit — that'll hurt *and* we don't have insurance yet."

I had been dreaming about her bicep when his words woke me up. 'Bite her?' I blushed. I felt like my mother had just walked in on me in full spank mode. How did these people know I wanted to bite Savannah — and Heavens to Murgatroid, didn't I just — and more importantly, why were they so *calmly* discussing it? And discussing me, as if I wasn't sitting there? I slammed my fork down. "What's going on?"

Buck pointed at me. "No. We'll talk about this later. First, we eat. Then, we go *outside* and smudge the shit out of this place. Then, you tell us what *you* know — then we'll see if we can help you. Then — and only then — we'll tell you what's going on.

Savannah clapped her hands. Her voice rose an octave, "And you might get to see me naked!"

John choked on his food as he broke out in hysterical laughter. His knee came up and bashed the underside of the table, making us all jump.

Dove got up, grumbled, and started clearing the table, even though no one had finished eating. Savannah was laughing now, too — there were tears in her eyes. Buck was moving his hands up and down trying to get everyone to calm down, but no one was heeding him.

"Okay, c'mon, get him out." Dove waved her hand at me like I was a smelly dog.

"C'mon, boy," Buck picked up a paper bag filled with newspaper that sat by the door. Was he going to roll a newspaper up and smack me with it?

When I stood, I actually felt my shameful doggy tail tuck between my legs. Without complaint, I followed Buck outside. He led me through the labyrinth of rose beds towards the front of the yard. When we were closer to the road than the house, we came upon a fire pit made of concrete blocks. It was surrounded by cheap aluminum lawn chairs with rusty joints.

"Have a seat, Sebastian, this'll take a while." He took a piece of newspaper out of the bag and crumpled it up into a ball. He threw the paper ball into the fire pit and started over with another piece of newspaper. There was a pile of twigs and small kindling already collected and waiting by the side of the pit. He arranged the sticks, then shook a match out of a box of kitchen matches.

Inside the house, Dove, Savannah and John walked back and forth by the windows, doing something, from one end of the house to the other. I thumbed the house. "What's up in there?"

They're cleaning it out — spiritually — performing a sacred ritual. I'm afraid you may have stunk us up, so we need to purify our home, to keep us safe.

Now Savannah was on the phone, talking animatedly. Dove reached for the pull chain that hung above the kitchen table. The ceiling fan whirred around slowly at first, then picked up speed. John kept disappearing and reappearing as he opened each window all along the front of the house.

I sat forward and put my hand on my chest. "I'm not the bad guy...I came here to tell you about the black energy that's scaring people in Peachtree." And there it was again, Angel's mangled body and my bite mark in her ass. "And something else."

Buck drew the match across the strike plate on the box. He lit four different sections of the pile of paper and kindling. When the fire caught, he said, "Your 'something else' and the black energy are the same thing, Sebastian." He stood up. "I need to get more wood. You stay put."

He returned soon enough, just appeared out of the darkness with an armful of birch logs. He let them fall to the ground then put three onto the growing fire. "They've got cedar, sage, sweetgrass, and...shit...be right back — I have to get them some tobacco or they're bound to get into my good Christmas Cheer stuff." He inspected me. "Now, you're going to stay put, right?"

I spread my arms wide, crossed my ostrich boots at the ankle and bellowed, "Where in the hell am I going to go?"

Buck stood over me. "Oh, you'll be going to hell, boy, and too soon, I'm afraid." He shook his head as he walked away. He yelled, "You stay. I'll be quick as a jiffy." Just before he went through the door of the house, he shouted at

176

the window, "Get outta my Christmas Cheer, woman! I told you before, use the triple-blend!"

I heard her tell him to 'hush it up.'

When Buck returned, he was wearing a jacket and his breathing was labored. "Whew! This is an exciting evening, isn't it?"

In the window, Dove was fanning the air with something.

Buck put some more logs on the fire and sat down in his creaky lawn chair. "Yup, she's smudging the place now. She burns the offerings to the Four Directions – East, North, South and West. Life begins in the East and ends in the North. When we burn, we invite the spirit to come and be with us. Sage gets rid of the negative spirits. She places the sage in an abalone shell, lights it, and fans the flames with a feather. The smoke is flowing over them, preparing them, protecting them. I'll have to go in soon and protect myself."

I guess what he had to say next was hard for him because suddenly he was addressing my boots. "You'll need a bit of a different ceremony...ah...so, for now, you sit back and enjoy the fire. Here, drink this." He reached into his deep, barn-coat pocket and handed me a Snapple bottle, clearly recycled, as the label was torn halfway off. The 'tea' inside was filled with sediment and leaves.

"What is this?"

"Protection disguised as shit water." He laughed. "Go ahead. Drink up — you're gonna need it." Then he was up and gone into the house again.

It seemed like forever before they all came outside. Buck was using a baseball bat as a cane and Savannah was in a bathrobe and bunny slippers. Oh, good Christ. I cleared my throat and imagined gnoshing on her ankles.

"Look at him — it's obvious he is affected. We don't really have to do this." Dove wrung her hands and sat down opposite me, on the other side of the fire. The fire shadow changed the features on her face, morphing her from middle-aged woman to goat to woman.

John snorted. "Ma, he could just be an average pig of a man, you know."

Dove mumbled. "Hmph — I know pig man and I know devil man...."

John was jovial as he put a video recorder on a short tripod and put the tripod on one of the cement blocks that surrounded the fire pit. He pointed the camera at me, pressed a button, and a red light came on to indicate that it was recording.

"I want to do this. I want to see it." Savannah's eyes were glazed, like she was staring at me, but didn't see me.

Dove sniffed. "Curiosity killed the cat." Everyone ignored her.

Savannah stood before me and John stood at her side. Ever so quietly, Buck walked around behind my chair.

Probably to support me for whatever weird-as-hell thing they were about to do.

Savannah whispered, "Sebastian, see here."

I looked up at her. Her eyes, they were so much like my Angel's eyes. My mouth watered. My tongue slid around my teeth.

She stood very rigid as she reached for the sash that held her robe closed.

My breathing hitched when I realized she was really going to do it, she was really going to open her robe and show herself to me. I groaned. I couldn't help it.

The sash was pulled away, the robe fell open, and there she was — all honey skin and full breasts with hardened brown nipples. Her waist curved in deep, which made her hips appear to flare wider. When my eyes rested on her pubis, I don't know what happened to me, but I let out a barking growl and made ready to jump at her, out of my chair. I heard Dove screech, "Now, Buck! Now!"

That's all I remember. The next morning, I woke up in a sleeping bag. I was still out by the fire, surrounded by empty bags of Cheetos and bottles of Sam Adams. Atop the fire ring, there was even a margarita glass with a little umbrella in it. I had the nastiest pain at the back of my head and a huge bump to go with it. What the hell had happened? Had there been a party out here while I was passed out? I gingerly touched the bump on the back of my head. I wasn't passed out; I was *knocked out*. And a margarita — they made me drink brown piss water, then they drank Sam Adams Harvest Pumpkin Ale and margaritas? I bet they were laughing their asses off in there over breakfast. I could smell ham. I raised my nose to the still morning air, maple ham — the sons of bitches.

When I reached the door, Dove came at me with her broom and shooed me out. "Oh, no you don't, you — I'll bring you a plate soon enough — though I don't know what for, you won't eat it, will you Dog-Devil-Eyes — no, you won't."

When she brought me a plate ten minutes later, I shoved the whole thick slab of Canadian bacon in my mouth and choked it down — just to show her. It was like leather; she had cooked it too long.

She rolled her eyes and called for Buck.

Buck came out of the house smelling fresh and clean. As he came down the step, he pulled on a crisp, white t-shirt. His braid was neat and he wore a leather hat with a string of shark's teeth around it. "How was your night, Dog-Devil-Eyes?"

"Yeah, okay — what's this about?"

"C'mon," he walked around the side of the house, and headed for the woods, "let's go for a walk and I'll tell ya."

Chapter 13

It was easy walking in his woods, there was a path first of all, which lead down to a lake, but also, it was a forest of pines — pines so thick they blocked the sun, so the forest floor wasn't choked with weeds. It was carpeted in old brown needles and smelled like Christmas.

"Do you remember anything from last night? I mean anything right before I knocked you out?"

I jumped back from him and held my poor head with both hands. "*You* knocked me out? What — with that bat?! Not cool, man, not cool!"

He kept walking and waved for me to keep up. "Do you know why you spent your last couple of weeks in Peachtree, Mr. Park?"

"They chose me. I don't know why they chose me." I picked up a stone and whipped it as far ahead of us as I could.

Buck erupted into an incredulous laugh that lacked humor. "Hell, yeah, you're the chosen one." He sighed, took off his hat and used his shoulder to rub the sweat from his temple. "You a ladies man, Sebastian?"

"I'm not a eunuch...."

"Humor me — how many women have you slept with?"

I gave him a blank stare.

This time, he laughed with genuine glee. "Okay. How many women have you slept with this month?"

I sniffed. "I don't know...seven...maybe eight...." I shrugged and sent a plume of pine needles into the air when I kicked at the forest floor. What was this line of questioning all about?"

"Ahhhhhh, that's what I thought."

Why was he smiling? Why had my statement made him so incredibly happy?

"Yes, Dog-Devil-Eyes, you're the chosen one." He looked at me. "How have your cravings been lately? Pancakes tasting bland? Cereal like sawdust? Fruit like wax? ...Meat not rare enough...?"

"Correct, correct — yeah, yeah, yeah...."

Buck stopped, took me by both arms, and pulled me around to face him. "Are you aware, Sebastian, that you are possessed?"

My knees buckled as I continued to stare at him. My eyes filled with tears as he looked at me encouragingly. Little moans escaped my lips as my breathing grew faster. He let his hands slide down my arms. He took both of my hands and he held them. I started to shake, to vibrate like an electrified convict. Buck squeezed my hands but I was a long way from being able to feel reassured.

"Here, come sit on this rock." He led me to a collection of massive boulders, all jumbled on each other. The topmost must've reached two stories high. We sat on the bottom-most; it was very broad and flat. "Didn't you know at all?"

I looked at him sheepishly. "Well, I knew something wasn't right, but jeez, I'm possessed...?"

He put his arm around my shoulders. "Yes, when we see vibrant young women, we, as men, should want to make love to them — not eat them...." He grinned.

My cheeks felt like they were burning. "I can't believe you're laughing this off...."

He hung his head. "Not at all, I'm not trying to diminish your suffering — only lighten it."

In the pine above us, I watched a starling dive bomb a squirrel. The squirrel dropped the nut or whatever he was carrying, did a flip on the branch, lost his grip, then fell to the forest floor with a plop. He scream-chittered at the starling and scampered off.

"Wow. I'm possessed." I put my head in my hands. "Why me?"

"Someone must have thought you were an easy target." Buck tugged on my shirtsleeve. I lifted my head. "Easy target? Who? What? Why?" Just before Buck spoke again, I felt a shift in the atmosphere around me and caught a whiff of ozone.

"You came to the Native Americans here, in this town...tell me why you didn't find anyone to talk to in Peachtree."

"There are no Native Americans in Peachtree — well, there are, they're not a clan, like you guys. No one talks about their Indianess over there."

"Exactly." Buck put his hat back on. "Many centuries ago, when the white men from across the sea were taking our land from us — they never had to fight us for Peachtree — we gave it to them. Matter of fact, no *good*, Great-Spirit-loving native has lived on that land, ever...."

"What are you saying?"

He held out his hands. "It's bad land, inhabited by an evil spirit long before man came to live on this Earth. It hunts mostly in Peachtree Forest, that stretch of pines that runs along Old Crabtree Road...."

"Yeah, well, there are some Native Americans living there."

"Yes, Sebastian, are you beginning to wake up now? Those that live there make deals with the evil spirit. They benefit from its black magic. They are its servants."

I thought of poor Mrs. Franklin and all of her physical suffering — if I was making a deal with the devil — I'd expect to get more than the shit end of the bargain that she appeared to be getting. I shook my head. "Nuh, uh. No, way — it doesn't make sense. I think I know the 'deal maker' you're referring to, and she's not getting any benefits from serving a devil." I told Buck about my visits to Mrs. Franklin. And didn't he just smile again. "What, Buck — why are you smiling like that?"

"I met Pamela Franklin once. It was many years ago. My father took me to Peachtree, to what he called 'a witch's funeral.' He told me we had to go, so I could see her face and know her. I was a frail kid and it was very difficult for me to walk to the casket and lay my eyes on my very first dead body. I had nightmares for many nights after that, and I was very afraid of the crows that pecked the button eyes out of

the scarecrow in my father's field. But, I wanted to be a man,

so I forced myself to stand on the kneeler and put my face

close to the dead witch that lay in the casket. I remember the

waxy smell of lilies — they still make me gag — and the

stench of chemicals. I smelled the Niagara Spray Starch that

someone had used to stiffen her blouse, the one with lace at

the throat. She had deeply wrinkled skin and a mole on her

right cheek. Her hair was thin and showed much of her

scalp."

"Yes, that's right, that's Pamela Franklin...but...."

"No, Sebastion, no." He waited for me to close my

gaping bottom lip. "That was Hettie Franklin. Her daughter

Pamela came up behind me, while I stood gawking on the

kneeler. I heard her voice hiss in my ear. 'You get out now,'

she told me and I almost lost my bladder. I turned around

quick to face her. She was the most beautiful white girl I had

ever met. She was like a seraphim angel, one of those

190

ethereal beings I saw on Christmas cards every December. She had golden hair all wound up in delicate ringlets and deep blue eyes, cold as the ice that grows on Moon Owl Lake." He shivered. "That beautiful angel slashed my heart with her evil eyes. I don't remember anything more after that. I was sick with the flu for the next three weeks. Well, we referred to it as the flu. My mother admonished my father for taking me there. But he told her that I must see the truth, and that I was strong enough."

It was statement-from-the-doofus time again, so I said, "I don't get it."

"This story has come full circle, Sebastian Park. My father showed me the face of Pamela Franklin all of those years ago so I could help you with your plight today. In exchange for aiding the evil spirit that dwells in the Peachtree Forest, Pamela Franklin doesn't have to die. When her body grows old, she gets a new shell, but only when she finds a new shell for the evil spirit."

191

"Oh, ho! New shells now, is it?" I jumped up and began pacing. I pointed at him. "I saw a picture of your so-called 'younger' Pamela on Mrs. Franklin's fridge — she told me it was her daughter."

"Yes, I'm sure that is her daughter."

I held my hands out to ask 'well???'

"And when Pamela finds a suitable body for the evil spirit, Pamela Franklin will be allowed to perform the ceremony to push her daughter's spirit out of her daughter's body. When the daughter's spirit is ostracized to the wind, Pamela will take over the girl's body and live another full life."

"No, way!" I was suddenly very clammy, standing there in the humid summer air. "How could she do such a thing? And to her own child?"

Buck put his head down. "She has been doing it for many centuries — giving birth to a girl child that she sends away and calls on only when the time is right."

"Holy shit — she never has boy children?"

"It is rumored that she feeds them to the beast."

At that, my stomach gurgled, my eyesight grew fuzzy and I fantasized about eating little babies, what with their sweet, fat limbs and intoxicating smell..... I slapped myself in the head and screamed, "Get out! Get out! Get out!"

Buck clapped at me to get my attention. "I will help you, Sebastian. I will fast and you will fast. We will prepare to rid you of this thing."

And now I was whining. "Why haven't you helped before this? Why do you let that thing do what it does?"

Buck spoke very low, "Did you let it do something horrific? Did you let it get away with it?"

Angel. Oh, Angel.

"The entity is an ancient, evil spirit. It is very powerful. It can only be appeased with sacrifices. We do not interfere except to educate our own and protect ourselves."

"Well, why don't you kill that fake old bitch?"

"You will see, on your inevitable return, that Pamela Franklin is well protected when physically threatened."

I kicked at the forest floor. "Shit!"

Buck got up. "Let's get to the house. At least we can cleanse you of this thing. Get you craving real chicken, instead of 'tastes-like-chicken'." He shook his head and walked away.

Chapter 14

When we got to the house, John yelled from the fire pit area, "Hey, you can't go in there!"

Buck climbed the step, turned around and winked at me. He shut the door so I wouldn't follow him into the house. I've been a dog all of my life, but this was the first time I actually felt like one. I spun on my heel and began to stalk towards John and the people he was with by the pit.

Behind me, Buck called from the window, "Hey, Dog-Devil-Eyes, drink this." He tossed me a bottle of water.

You'll need lots of that to defeat evil, so drink plenty of it over the next couple of days. And for love of the Great Spirit, do not, I repeat — *do not* — take a bite out of someone or eat someone. Once you have consumed human flesh — once you have actually swallowed it — the thing can come and claim your body. It will run your body to its hunting grounds, with your spirit still in there somewhere, and use you to eat the flesh it craves. Then you will be lost to us — we will not be able to help you." He moved to the door and quickly let out a couple of small, brown dogs, then pressed the door firm to his body — as if I was trying to get in. Pfft. "Go with the others now."

I was in full sulk when I reached the pit and in no mood to meet John's two friends who were guffawing behind their hands and staring at me in pure circus-act merriment. Savannah sat quietly in the chair where I had sat the night before. She was wearing baggy sweats and had a blanket around her shoulders. Her pupils were so dilated I could see my stooped reflection in them. I sighed – I was a lover, not a biter.

"Damn, Brother — we've been watching this shit for an hour — good show!" John pointed to the small TV on top of the wall of the fire pit. Three end-to-end extension cords led to the house. The camcorder was hooked up to the television and I saw my face frozen on the screen. "We brought the TV out here so you could watch this, Dog-Devil-Eyes."

I sat down hard in a folding chair — not near Savannah, her sweet scent was too tantalizing. John started the video. The face, there, on the screen, was supposed to be me, but it wasn't my face. I was acting weird — not blinking enough and my jaw seemed stiff or something. "I don't look like that."

Savannah cleared her throat. "Yes, you do."

The camera had been shooting at me from behind Savannah, so in the film, we saw the back of Savannah, and me beyond her. Watching her. And *drooling*. Intense heat crawled up the nape of my neck and burned my ears. I felt Savannah's eyes on me — watching me watch her. In the video, she opened her robe.

John's friends' hoots were quickly stunted when John reached over and slapped the dumber-looking one up the side of his head.

I watched me in the video and saw how my face contorted as I salivated over Savannah's naked body like a fiend. The skin on my face actually tightened and bloated as if it was breathing on its own. In the video, when I leaned forward to study her crotch, my eyes came into the firelight and I saw what they had all grown silent over...my eyes were black — I mean, jet-black — big, black grapes wobbling in my eye sockets. When I made the attempt to leap like a feral cat, Dove yelled, 'Now, Buck! Now!' Out of the blackness behind me, the baseball bat swung and stopped with a crack behind my head. Then there was more screaming and yelling and snow — end of video.

The others were staring at me.

The dumber-looking friend said, "Yeah, you're not coming into my house, either."

***

For the next couple of days, I starved, which was no big deal because my appetite had dwindled to almost nothing anyway. When someone from one of the seven families was available, they babysat me — outside. I wasn't allowed to be alone with small, fat children or sexy women — on account that it was known that those two types of people, those two temptations, could aggravate my 'condition.' It was decided that minimum security would work for me and that I could be of use while I hung around doing my fasting. First, I sat outside Buck's door at the family picnic table and Dove attempted to teach me the fine art of basket weaving. (I sucked at it. As far as I know, none of my 'monster baskets' ever made it to the gift shop that the families owned and operated in town.) Dove was a well-known basket maker, as in — I've-got-a-piece-in-the-Museum-of-Fine-Arts-in-Boston, well-known. She took me on hikes to gather the materials she used — black ash and sweet grass — then tried her hardest to teach me how to weave the shit. My dexterous hands, the fingers that had delighted hundreds with their swift bra removal, just couldn't get the hang of basket weaving.

I was shuffled over to Dumber's house — yes, I eventually learned his name, but I already forgot it. Aaron? Baron? Daryn? I don't know. All seven families pitched in to collect maple sap from their trees, but it was Dumber's family that cooked the sap into maple syrup and formed the maple candies. They told me it was the Indians who first discovered how to cook maple when maple tree sap from a broken limb dripped into a man's fire and gave off a wonderful aroma. While we made the rounds checking tubes, taps, and buckets, Dumber's old mother — who smelled horrifically of B.O. and patchouli — asked me if I had a woman named Sophie related to me. I told her I did. She told me that Sophie had come to her in a dream and said that she was protecting me, and that's why I was still alive.

"Tell her I said, 'thank you very much'." I walked into a bucket of sap and knocked the thing to the ground.

B.O.-Patchouli squinted at the tipped-over bucket. (If they were going to give me a shitty Indian name, I was going to give some of them shitty Indian names....) She watched the sap run into the ground with a dried-prune-face grimace. "Tell her yourself, dumb ass."

I was shuffled to the next house.

At night, when I wasn't busy working or busy being heckled or busy being the heckler, I camped out by the fire and grew small and afraid. What was this thing inside me?

Was it really there, or were these people a bunch of

fruitcakes? Was I really with the good guys now, or what?

Could they get the thing out of me? And how would they do

it? Would they drown it out of me or draw-and-quarter it

out of me like they did to the Salem witches — this was New

England, after all, and they were guilty of some highly

questionable methods of exorcism over the years. Exorcism.

I never watched the whole movie, *The Exorcist,* I was too

scared, and now that was going to be me, supposedly. I

wanted to run. But, I stayed there, on the cold ground,

waiting for the next day. Because I knew, that thing *was*

definitely inside of me. I could feel it waiting. I could hear it

whispering to me. I remembered how it happened — that

first night at Rog's when I had the dream about the small,

black smoke ball at my window. I remembered opening the

window and having that foul, black thing shove itself down

my throat. I cringed every time I thought of it. Talk about

needing to keep your big mouth shut. So, the people here

were right, Pamela Franklin had set that thing on me on the very first night — only it hadn't won, they hadn't won — not yet.

It took eight days of meditation before Buck felt ready to attempt a try at me. He didn't appear any worse for the weight loss — he was still a rugged guy — but I was verging on skeletal and almost resembled that creature that murdered Angel out in the woods. I needed help, quick.

Chapter 15

We made a procession out to the woods, down towards the lake, and stopped at the cluster of boulders. It was around noon, the time when the good spirits of the forest took had dominance, and the bad spirits waited for darkness to gain strength. The people chanted all the way down the path, and two of them at the back played drums. Buck was in full buckskin costume with headdress and all. Some of the others wore their powwow clothes, too — kinda like going to church in your Sunday best. I was feeling more than a little insane. Before we arrived at the rocks, I suddenly screamed like a laboring hyena. I don't know where the outburst had come from — I certainly hadn't ordered it.... I slapped my hand to my mouth and tried to smother the scream to a stop.

Buck came over to me. "It knows what we are doing. It screams through you. It knows we are not afraid and it knows we have the power to banish it from you. You are weak. Not in spirit, but in body. You have made your body weak so it cannot use you against us. This makes it weak. We will deliver it from you." He walked to the head of the procession and headed for the rocks.

I felt a pain in my gut — a force that drove at the wall of my skin like a spike. I screamed again, but this time no one stopped to watch.

Dumber's mother was at my side. She took my hand and whispered, "These boulders form the gate to a complex cave system that has been used as a magic place for thousands of years. You will see when you enter and descend to the womb of the rock, there are paintings in there and script in an indecipherable language. It is a special place with strong power. Good power. You will be okay." She squeezed my fingers.

When I got to the entrance, my body jerked back. I stumbled and fell and expected to crack my head on the rock that I knew was behind me. Instead, I felt many hands at my legs, buttocks, back and cupped at my head — several people had reached out to catch me.

After Dove steadied me, she took her hands away and rubbed them together like she was ridding herself of dirt. "It is trying to damage your body."

I suddenly felt completely exhausted. The entrance to the cave was jagged and dark. "I'm terrified — I can't go in there."

"It is manipulating you. The real Sebatian Park would never be afraid to go into that hole." Buck pointed to the flat boulder. "Here, sit for only a minute — then we're going in. But we must get this thing out of you now, Sebastian."

The group spread out around me, sat down, and murmured amongst themselves.

"When you get this thing out of me, when it can't take over my body — what will it do then?" A new pain started in my spine, like something was prodding me with a hot iron.

"It will roam the town and hunt for a new vessel. Most of the people in town know a version of an old folktale that tells them not to open their mouths to the black ghost. As for food, if Mrs. Franklin does not provide for it, it will provide for itself, which means anyone and everyone in town will be at risk not only of possession, but also as food."

I held my hand up and tried to catch my breath. "Wait a minute, she's the one who decides what it eats?"

"Yes, mostly — unless she does not appease it, then it decides what it eats."

"Shee-it." I held my aching gut, which was starting to feel like a bowl of fire. "How on Earth does she have control over it in the first place?"

Buck shrugged. "She's a witch — she summoned it. Summoned it and bid it to grant her one desire...the ability to possess. It was able to give this to her — that is its greatest power. A pact between a witch and a demon strengthens both of their powers. That is why we are together here, today — there is strength in numbers."

Some of the men in the group replied to his comment with yips and howls, making us sound like a pack of coyotes.

"We must do this now, Sebastian; we don't have much time before nightfall."

"Nightfall? That's over seven hours away.... How do we not have enough time?"

Buck shook his head. "This is the ten-course meal of exorcisms, Sebastian, not Burger King. We have to go now."

It caused me a lot of pain to stand up straight. So much so, that I collapsed. John and Dumber quickly came to my side and helped me up. They slung my arms around their necks and dragged me into the cave. Most of the people stayed outside. They still chanted and beat on the drums. We had to crouch while we advanced. As we walked down the steep, rocky decline I started screaming. Nonstop. It was weird because I was conscious that I was screaming when I didn't want to, and I was embarrassed at the same time that I was enraged. Only, I wasn't really enraged, I knew that, but the thing inside of me was extremely enraged and it was pressing on my emotional buttons. I felt bad for the people around me who had to listen to that caterwauling, and then I felt even worse when my fingernails grew, actually grew as I stared at them, and felt mortified when I took both of my hands and tried to scratch at the faces of John and Dumber. I heard Buck yell, "Get the ropes!" Suddenly, there were hands all around me again, only this time they weren't helping me up; they were holding me down and tying me up. I didn't think they really needed to tie me up — I was weaker than ever. Not only could I not lift a finger, but my eyes were heavy and I just wanted to pass out.

After they had me rope-swaddled, they strapped me to a hand truck with bright orange ratchet straps and pushed me forward through the dimly lit cave — which was way beyond humiliating. I was glad no one was filming the whole thing. That's when I saw John out of the corner of my eye, motioning frantically to Dumber's brother. With my eyes at half-mast I looked at the brother — he had John's camera fixed on my face. Fucking kids.

The next several hundred feet were uneventful, save for the fart that ripped out of my ass and threatened to drop everyone right there, dead from toxic fumes.

John waved the air in front of his face. His eyes were watering. "Eeeeew. Gct-damn, Dad — are you gonna make this dude pay for services rendered after this shit or what?"

Buck answered, as mellow as ever. "It is the demon, John, ignore it and it will stop that tactic."

John guffawed and poked me with his walking stick. "*Ignore it* — shit, how the hell are we supposed to ignore it?"

More air blasted out of me. I didn't think it was funny because it actually sliced out of my ass and hurt like hell. There was another wave of complaining in the tight tunnel and much gagging.

We emerged into a small room with a sloped ceiling. What was left of the party held back except for Buck, Dove, John, and me — the monster. They wheeled me to the center of the room, tipped me back, rolled me off the hand truck and placed me in a supine position in the center of the room. They set up candles in a circle around me and as they lit them, my body began to writhe. On the walls I could see the pictures and strange writing that B.O.-Patchouli had mentioned. It was fascinating. Without warning, another scream erupted out of me. It was a screech, really, and there was such force behind it. I tasted blood.

Buck began to pray. And to chant. And to chant and pray. "Oh, Great Spirit, hear your people's call. Fill us with your light...."

A high-pitched garbled voice spoke — out of me. It kind of sounded like a representative of the Lollipop Guild while he was being strangled. But the stuff it spewed sounded more like the fodder from the Tourette's Guild. I like to swear — I'm not perfect — but the shit this demon was saying was pure filth. Disgusting. You get the picture. The next sensation I was privy to felt like ten million little bugs had spread out over my body and were pulling every hair follicle from my scalp, all the way down to my big toes — and the ones on the toes are really sensitive. They didn't pull my hairs out, just applied constant strain. This time, when the scream came, it was really me.

Time went on. I begged Buck to stop praying. With every word he uttered my pain escalated. Buck shook his head sadly at me and kept right on praying. If I had known the pain was going to be this bad, I would've just drunk myself to death. Buck and Dove probably knew this and that's why they didn't tell me what they had planned. There was no preparing for this.

Sometimes, I passed out, but the thing woke me repeatedly with acid blasts of a shitty taste shot through my nose and mouth, and left me choking. That feeling melted into a drowning sensation. For several horrible seconds I thought I was drowning. I thrashed and struggled in my ropes like a huge maggot. That's when I heard the slithering. I turned my head. One of my eyes was swollen shut, but out of my good eye I could see snakes coming at me across the dusty rock floor.

"Snakes! Snakes! Snaaaaakes." I tried to make Buck look at me while I lay there defenseless in ties that he had ordered, but his head was bowed and his eyes were closed as he kept on chanting. The snakes had fangs that dripped with venom. They moved impossibly fast. They were on me in two seconds, slithering up my clothes and twining around my neck. Again, I was choking. My breathing stopped and only a high-pitched squee of air escaped from my throat.

Dove slapped my face. "Those snakes aren't really there! You're not really being strangled — stop that! You're hurting yourself!"

And then I felt like a victim of the cannibal monster. I started feeling bites taken out of me, all over my body. My toes were bitten off and my kneecaps and fingers. Something licked out my eyeballs and gnawed at my nose. I felt claws scratch my back and rake across my stomach and then, too much to bear, I felt my penis being tugged before it was bitten through and ripped off my body. Throughout it all, I screamed, screamed, screamed.

Then there was a moment when the world stopped. I couldn't see anything, feel anything, or see anything. I was in a space of black that felt more empty than any place I'd ever been. There was a whoosh of air. Suddenly, I felt light as the air that surrounded me. I felt light in me, and I felt light run through my pores. I could taste the light — it was cool and clean. I opened my good eye. John was trying not to cry. Dove was moaning as she lay sprawled over Buck. On the cave floor, Buck was motionless.

Chapter 16

It took many men to get Buck's body safely out of the cave. He was running a fever and his skin was bloated and shiny. They struggled to get him up to the house. On instruction given to John by Buck just before the evil spirit left me, I was taken down to the lake to wash in the pre-dawn hours for a cleansing ritual. As I stood naked and shivering in the lake, with half the clan regarding me in silence, Dumber began to chant in a high, girly voice that lulled me till I broke down and cried. I knelt in the water and splashed frigid waves over my shoulders. How was I ever going to go back to Peachtree and defeat the thing in its large form — I didn't think I could walk up the hill without dying. Then I realized what I just thought — I was planning on going to Peachtree to defeat that thing.

Why did I plan on something so stupid? Really, I could have just taken off, hightailed it to New Mexico after breakfast. I assumed that it was a new drive that I had in me. A drive as strong as my sex drive and my hunger drive and my protection drive. It was just something I had to do. Maybe I did it for selfish reasons — just the way I did everything in my life. Maybe I was afraid of Angel's ghost and wanted to put her to rest by getting rid of the thing. Or maybe, hallelujah, I wanted to do a good thing and avenge a nice girl's death. Maybe my manly pride was bruised because an old lady was going to best me if I ran away. I just don't know. I don't think about that anymore.

Up at the house, things were quiet. The ambulance had already come and gone and taken Buck, Dove, and John with them. Savannah was cooking pancakes. I came through the door, gauged my reaction upon seeing her ankles, and relaxed when I was sure that I didn't want to eat her. I sat down at the table. "I don't think I can eat that." It had been so long since I'd had a full meal that I really didn't want one. The very thought made me nauseous.

"Just try a little," she said in her soft voice. I could tell she was stressed out, with her thick, wavy hair falling out of her clips and the way she kept checking the rooster clock that hung crooked on the wall.

I tried a little. It got stuck in my throat, then I threw up on my plate. I swallowed back the last of the acid that accompanied it. "There you go then."

"Oh, you..." She tossed the paper plate with vomit in the trash and put her hands on her hips. "Now, they said you probably wouldn't be able to stomach much, so I'm going to skip to the last resort and make you a chocolate protein shake. You're lucky Daryl (*That* was 'Dumber's' name) is on his Schwarzenegger kick, or whatever, we don't usually have protein shakes laying around here. I want to get some nutrients in you, then tuck you into bed so I can go to the hospital and check on all of them. I'm really worried." She reached up and released her hair. As soon as it tumbled down, she gathered it up, twisted it, and clipped it again.

"Gimme the protein drink — I'll try." I kept a couple of sips down, but stopped when I knew my body really wouldn't take anymore. (Over the next week, I was able to take more and more protein shake. I finally graduated to whole foods on the seventh day.) She took me to a crudely attached addition at the back of the house. Light from the outside leaked through the wall seams. There were three sets of triple bunks, all strewn with mismatched sheets, and handmade quilts and afghans. There was a wood burning stove in one corner. The room was like a tent with wooden walls, and it suited me just fine. Rain started outside, quick and hard. I hopped on a bunk and Savannah tucked a quilt around me. I was so happy to be able to rest, I almost wept.

Buck was dying.

I rattled around in his home for a week until I grew stronger. I visited him at the hospital, sometimes with Dove, and sometimes with John and Savannah, but his condition was always the same — he didn't wake up, his fever persisted.

One night, Dove came to stand by me. She leaned close and whispered, "It's time for you to return to Peachtree. This thing has hold of my Buck and won't let him go. You need to help him. First, return to my home. Go into the top drawer of my bureau, on the right. You'll see a grey-skinned pouch. Put it on — it will protect you. Then, go to Daryl's father, he will tell you how to fight the demon." She stood up and held her arms open. I hugged her hard. I never saw her or Buck again.

Daryl's father was a weird dude. B.O.-Patchouli let me in with a grunt when I knocked on the door of their double-wide. And, Lord have mercy, didn't the B.O. and patchouli smell just intensify tenfold. I longed for Rog's clean home and Cat Ass at my feet. I took a peek inside the abode. It screamed of 'packrat.'

"I'll just wait outside, if it's all the same to you."

She shrugged. "Don't bother me, you little snot." She shut the door in my face. This was the same woman who held my hand when I was possessed.

Daryl's father, Long-Feather, came jittering and jangling outside like he was a human livewire. He was tall and gangly, with perpetually excited pop-eyes. He shook my hand. "Glad to see you doing better — putting some weight on, I see, huh?"

And before I could answer....

"They ever tell you what you were up against?"

And before I could answer....

"That thing out there, it's a certain type of demon — a Wendigo — ever heard of it?"

I didn't try to answer.

He sat down at his picnic table and told me to do the same. "Now, I'll tell you what all about the Wendigo and you tell me if any of this rings true...."

I stared at him.

"Now see, the Wendigo is an evil spirit that lives in the woods." He jumped around on the bench as he spoke. "It craves human flesh so it wants to possess a human and use him as a tool — as a way to eat the human flesh. He can't possess a human unless the human has already tasted human flesh. You see that there? That's where you got your catch-22."

I raised my eyebrows.

He laughed. "Yeah, ain't that the bird?" He waved his hands all around as he spoke. "Can't use a human to eat a human unless the human has already tasted human!" He slapped the table and 'bwhahahahahaaed.'

I cleared my throat.

"So, what he has to do then is *tempt* the human to eat the human — that's where you came in, see? There must've been something weak about your spiritual self, pardon me, that allowed him to easily slip inside and navigate your mind. But hey, don't get too down — you weren't so weak that he could get you to do what he wanted. You were only *mildly* weak, and now, I'd say, you're a shitload stronger!"

"Yeah,buthowcanIdefeatit?" I knew I had to talk quick, if I was going to get a sentence in.

He took a breath, was about to talk, then, "Come again?"

I eyed him hard. Would he really let me speak? I opened my mouth to see if he'd cut me off.

He gave me the what's-wrong-with-you-boy look.

"How can I defeat it?"

He shrugged and raised his eyebrows. "Get rid of the old lady — that won't be easy — trap the thing, torture it with prayer, and banish it to a realm where it can't harm anyone. Basically, tell the bully to get the hell out. It has no right to do what it's doing — tell it that." He put his hands in his pants pockets, wiggled his fingers, and made some coins sing. "That's how you get rid of a demon!"

I rolled my eyes. "Really? That's it?" I know a whole bunch of people who torture themselves with prayer every Sunday who don't seem to be improving at all. How the hell was prayer going to get this thing to behave?

"Did Cooing-Dove give you the salt?"

"What? No."

He bounced around on the bench. Why didn't he just get up and turn a couple of somersaults? "Cooing-Dove didn't tell you to get her salt pouch out of her bureau drawer?"

"What? This? Yeah, I got it." I pulled the pouch out from under my shirt where it hung on a long, leather cord.

"Yeah, yeah — gimme that." He took the pouch from me and opened it. He showed me its contents. "See, this here is salt. Special salt. Strong stuff. Purified and blessed. You can sprinkle it around your demon to trap him in one spot so you can say your prayers and force it away with your will."

"With my will...." I stared at the salt. "I'm going to trap it with salt and force it away with my will."

"Yes, sir. It will be able to disappear to another realm, but it will not be able to leave that circle." He drew the sack closed and handed it to me. He reached across the picnic table and tapped me on the head. "Only if you believe."

I took the salt bag and put its leather cord over my head. I tucked the bag inside my button-down shirt. Behind a t-shirt, it would appear like I was wearing my heart outside of my skin. At the time, looks were the farthest thing from my mind. It was a sad miracle.

Long-Feather got up, came around the picnic table and offered his hand. "Surround yourself with white light, Brother, prepare yourself. Call on those souls that surround you. They can help you, strengthen you. You need to believe this."

I nodded and shook his hand. He hugged me and patted my back.

Early the next morning, I said my goodbyes to a couple of the other folks then packed up what little I had brought with me and drove out the gate as John held it for me. I pulled into *The Black Chicken* parking lot, drove around back, and tossed my fake ghost hunting equipment in the Dumpster. I stalked into the store and gave that sassy girl one long, hard stare. She nodded and led me to the back room.

"What's your name darlin'?" I breathed in her ear as I pulled her shirt up over her head.

"Coco," she whispered and fumbled with my belt as my Stetson toppled off my head and bounced on the dirty floor. I took her in with all of my senses and I thanked the powers that be over and over again that I wanted to make love to her, not eat her. When we were done we clung to each other.

"Will you come back?" She had the most beautiful liquid-electric eyes.

I held her tight. "I'll try my hardest." And this time, I meant it.

Chapter 17

On the way home, I thought about the mayor and his creepy-ass son. What was their deal? How did they fit into all of this? I figured the son was kind of innocent and didn't really understand that he was stealing from people who had just been murdered — his eyes were void of all emotion that would have betrayed him as guilty. His father, the mayor, however, sure as hell knew what was going on. Otherwise, Junior would never get away with having all of that shit in his barn. Nevermind that, Junior couldn't ever afford a barn

— someone had made it possible for him to have that barn.... So, what was the mayor getting out of it? Why did he cover up the fact that people were being eaten alive in his town? And what about that Patricia woman, the broad that was at Pamela's house the night Pamela and I got back from that worthless stakeout? I didn't like her from the get-go and she *was* the one who told me to go hiking on Old Peachtree Road — the demon's hunting grounds. The wretch, did she tell *all* of the tourists to go hiking on Old Peachtree Road?

What about Rog? Was he okay? It made my heart heavy to think that he had anything to do with this. I went with my gut — my gut told me 'no.' And what about Angel? Why did no one worry about Angel when she wasn't at work the next day? I smelled Coco on me and knew I'd go back for her. If she wasn't at work, I'd find out where she was — I'd search for her until I found her. Was there no one in the world that would look for Angel? I just couldn't believe that. I held the steering wheel with both hands. I was squeezing it so hard my fingernail beds were white. I pressed the accelerator and passed the car in front of me even though we were in a no-pass zone. The guy stuck his hand out the window and chucked me the bird. I drove faster. I boiled with indignant rage. Pussified Peachtree had some splainin' to do.

When I pulled into the diner, it was late-breakfast time and the place was over-crowded as usual. I drove right up to the front door, and even though it wasn't a parking spot, I put the Bug in park and shut off the engine. I shoved my door open, left it open, slammed through the diner's double doors, and stood in the middle of the restaurant. I held my arms out like I was the second coming and brought them all to an instant shut up.

"Good people of Peachtree. Remember me?" As I scanned the crowd, the crowd looked away — almost like doing the wave by lowering the eyes. I walked up to an elderly couple in the booth closest to me. "Mrs. McGurtry, remember me?" Mrs. McGurtry's face turned red under her badly cut bangs. She made eye contact with her husband then picked up her fork and started poking her pecan pancakes. I leaned down and whispered in her ear, "Now, c'mon honey, it hasn't been that long since I've been to the post office."

I went down the aisle to a booth in the back. "Ladies...." I gave a mock bow to the table of five women. They all worked at *The Farm Emporium*. They seemed very worried — very *guilty*...why was that? I spun around.

"I don't claim to know everything — so you may have to help me out here — but I'll tell you what I know." I paused again. I should have just gone into theater, then none of this would have ever happened. "I know that some of you think I should be dead by now." There were a couple of gasps, but I couldn't tell from whom. I gave a big, fake laugh and held up my hands to do the 'quote-unquote' thing. "Well, hahaha, not 'dead' more like, 'possessed'." This drew an even bigger

231

response — some gasps, some cries, some throat clearing. Two people I didn't know got up and headed for the exit.

"Go ahead now, I know where you live…"

"Screw you," the man yelled back.

I raised my eyebrows and tsk-tsked. "You know where anger comes from, right everyone? It comes from fear. Anyone else here *angry* that I'm standing before you now and am quite openly confronting you? The restaurant had grown completely silent again. I heard gum snap behind me. I turned around to face Angel's complacent replacement. Her no-nonsense stance told me she wanted to paddle me for harassing the other kids.

"Honey, you know I'm gonna call the cops, right? The way you're actin' right now is just not right…."

"I'm just talking," I put my face close to her chest to read her nametag, "Ella…just talking. Give me two more minutes then I'll leave you all alone." She shook her head and started to walk in the direction of the kitchen. "Oh, and Ella?"

She turned, crossed her arms over her chest, and frowned.

"Where's Angel?"

Ella rolled her eyes.

I spoke to the entire restaurant. "No, really. Where's Angel? You know Angel — the pretty girl that used to waitress here...Does anyone know?" Some people scowled at me, some hung their heads. "Because I know where Angel is...." I swear someone took a giant's vacuum cleaner, turned it on, and sucked all of the oxygen right out of that room. Now they were *all* gawking at me. I nodded and scratched my chin. "Not three weeks ago, our Angel was chewed alive by a tall ugly monster that lives in Peachtree Forest...." I expected the room to explode with voices. I felt the sensation of snails slime down my spine when — it didn't. A couple of families with kids got up and herded their young out, but that was it. So, I went on.

"Yeah, that black entity you supposedly called me to get rid of? It's a ghost all right." I slapped myself in the forehead. "Well, it's actually a *demon,* boys and girls, and it likes to put on a human body once in a while and eat other human bodies." That's it, that got 'em talking. Talking, screaming, cursing, crying, blaming — you name it. There was even a short-lived brawl in the back right quadrant.

"This is heinous, people...*heinous!* Which of you has been covering up for this thing? Why have you been covering up for this thing? What the hell is going on in Peachtree?"

Ella came over and started shoving me towards the door. "Okay, Sunshine. that's it. Out you go. I'll give you a five minute head start before I call the police."

When I went out the second of the two diner doors I found one of the families with the small kids waiting by my Bug.

The husband stepped towards me. "I-I-I don't know if this helps or nothin'..." He glanced at his wife. She pretended sudden interest in her fingernails. "...my brother used to get tea from that old Franklin woman — used to tell us it was magic and all. But you gotta understand, my brother was a free-lovin' ton-tokin' hippie jackass. I mean, he did *a lot* of shit."

His woman took the two kids by the hands and pulled them a little ways off, to stand and sulk under a pine tree on the other side of the parking lot. Her husband put his hands in his jeans pockets.

"One night he comes over my house sayin' the old lady wouldn't give him any more tea unless he went into the woods to talk to the trees. So, he says he goes into the woods, was walkin' down Old Crabapple Road when this

235

black smoke comes up to him and surrounds him. Makes him want to puke his guts out. So, he's sitting at my table crying and tells me, ever since then he's been wanting to go too far when he's munchin' on his old lady, if you know what I mean..."

I kept my face blank.

"Yeah, he's crying and crying, talking about witches and devils and I was pretty sure he was just taking a bad trip till the next day, when they find his body floating face-down in Willow Pond. They open him up, to figure if it was murder or suicide, and they find his entire body, all his insides coated in black — like black soot — all over his insides. So, I've heard weird shit whispered around this town before, one thing being 'you mess up, you get fed to the devil,' and another thing being that lots of folks think that Franklin's an old witch. I don't know, after my brother died, I just pay a little more attention to all that shit, is all."

He watched his little family. "Sometimes I think of movin', you know? But, it's like, if you watch your step around here, and don't ask too many questions, this is the safest town in the world. Like I can tell you for a fact — my kids can walk the streets in this town and not get picked up by any pervs or whatever. We just don't take them hiking around here. But lately, we've been talking about moving again because this is the first time people been seeing that black cloud *out of the woods*. I've lived here all my life and we've always been afraid of the demon in the woods. But shit, now that there have been sightings around town, like, real accounts, ya know? It just don't feel safe anymore."

I winced. "Haven't the town sightings been going on for over a year?"

He shrugged. "Well, yeah. But, I don't know, otherwise, it's so *safe* here — you know?"

No. I didn't know. Idiot. I shook his hand. "Thank you, Mr...."

"I'm Chezzy."

"Well, thanks, Chezzy — that was enlightening."

"Yeah, whatever." He yelled to his family, "Let's go!" and the kids tromped over to him like two released puppies.

I got into the Bug and headed for the Ox Blood. I don't know what I expected to happen when I got out of the Bug, concerning Mrs. Franklin and all, but nothing did happen. I mean, I felt like I was being watched as I pulled into the driveway and chose a parking spot. But that was either because I was paranoid or because Cat Ass was waiting for me on his chair in the window. He ran over to me as soon as I was through the door, and I let him rub himself on me, poor little bugger.

"Where the hell have you been?" Rog lumbered towards me over the old, complaining floor boards, got into my personal space and loomed over me, all red-faced and huffy.

Oh, man. "I've been doing research — I lost track of time...."

He bellowed, "Casper, even from you, that's a lame excuse."

"I swear — lots of research, and I got sick. It was all that puking that held me up for days."

"I went out there, you know, to that Indian reservation...."

"It's not a reservation...."

"And the gate was locked. LOCKED! I didn't know what to do. I got so pissed I just took off. I figured, if you wanted to stay there, well, you could bloody well stay there!"

"Ai yi yi..." How did this turn into me 'placating the girlfriend?' "Rog! I was sick! I couldn't come back right away, but I'm here now."

Suddenly, he rushed at me and almost killed me in a bear hug. When he backed off he said, "Mrs. Franklin missed you too — she's been asking about you."

I cringed. "What did you tell her?"

His face flushed again. "That you were off playing cowboys and Indians — what was I supposed to tell her?" He walked away, grumbling to himself.

Great. The old witch *must* suspect where I went and she must suspect why. I went over to the window and spied on her house from behind the curtain. It seemed the same as ever. There was a white Corolla in her yard. I followed Rog into the kitchen. "Hey, whose Corolla is that next door?"

Rog was stacking the dishwasher. "That's Mrs. Franklin's daughter — came up from South Carolina to meet her mother for the very first time. Mrs. Franklin had to give the girl up — no one is really sure why. Mrs. Franklin guards her privacy."

"Mmmm hmmm." I watched him. He was smiling now — his blustery moments never lasted long. He was smiling because Mrs. Franklin's daughter had come up to visit the poor old girl. How could I tell him that Pamela

Franklin had the girl come up so she could take over the girl's body? I couldn't. I was going to let him live in his dream world as long as possible. He looked so happy.

"Say, Rog? What's that tea that Mrs. Franklin makes — can I buy it in town?"

"Well, sure. Which kind you want? I have some here."

Could I possibly be that lucky? "Well, let's see what you got..."

We went to the pantry and he showed me jars of jasmine tea, chamomile tea, black tea — lots of tea. None of it smelled like grass cuttings and old tennis shoes. That was the stuff I wanted to find. That had to be the 'magic tea'. Now that I thought about it, I was too interested in her pot of tea that day. I should have trusted my interest and discovered *why* I was interested in it. "Hmmm, I'm don't think this is the tea I'm looking for."

Roger narrowed his eyes. "You haven't asked for any tea since you've been here — what are you up to?"

I feigned innocence.

He rolled his eyes. "Hot damn, boy — you're such a bad actor. What is it? You been listening to those jamokes in town about her 'magic tea'?" He waited for me to own up to my sneakiness. "Yeah, uh-huh, you're squirming! Now you see here, I do believe our old girl is making some tea that may not be on the up and up. And I do believe we got some here in town drinking the shit, including that fool mayor, who could get in big trouble for taking such a risk. But, I also believe she doesn't mean anyone any harm — she's just an old girl who still calls drugs 'medicine' as opposed to the newer, uglier word 'narcotics'."

I raised my eyebrows. "Really!"

"Yut, now that's between you and me. I only told you because I trust you and I don't want you going around and

242

turnin' up already tilled soil. And you don't need any magic tea, so leave well enough alone."

I needed to get my hands on that tea. I picked my Stetson up off the kitchen table where I had tossed it. "I'm going to town — need anything?"

I went to the gift shop district. That means I went to the seven shops at the end of Stadler Street, just off of Main. I pushed on the heavy, carved wooden door to the apothecary shop. When it gave way, I caught a whiff of B.O.-Patchouli — the initial waft of herb scent bowled me over, but I quickly blocked that out and presented myself to the limp young man behind the counter. He put his magazine down and smirked.

"Well, well, Shakespeare — I heard about your protestations at the diner this morning. Ghosties and ghoulies, is it?"

I ignored that. "I'd like some of Mrs. Franklin's special tea. I was told you definitely could get me some." I fished a twenty out of my pocket and slid it across the counter with an eyebrow wiggle.

His pursed his lips as he placed his index finger on the bill and slid it onto his lap. He leaned forward and whispered, "Well, you heard wrong." He made a twirl on his high barstool. "Can I give you a sample of her jasmine tea? It's wonderfully entitled *Calm Sunshiny Day*."

I stood up straight. "Really? You're not going to help me?"

He stood up too. "I can help you with jasmine tea."

"I was told you were cool — that you were the man to see."

"And I can help you with chamomile tea...."

"Yeah, I gotcha." I stomped back out into the sunshine, pissed as all hell and at a loss.

"Wotcha doin' cowboy?"

It was the mayor's assistant. She was strolling down the street eating an ice cream cone.

244

"Oh, you know — struggling for a clue, as usual."

She stopped when she reached me. She had an I-know-something-you-don't-know smile shining on her face. "Guess what I just heard?"

I pinched her arm. "Oh, let me guess — I was bitching about hoogity boogities at *Ma's Breakfast* this morning."

She bonked her ice cream on my nose, leaving a black raspberry smudge there. "You got it." She wiped the ice cream off my nose with her napkin.

"Well, I have even more trouble now — I'm getting ready to leave town, packing up and all, and I realized I must've lost my gold cufflink in the mayor's office during our last meeting, you know, playing Ping-Pong. Those cuff links are so special to me, handed down to me from my mother when she died, who got them from her father when he died." Then I hung my head and looked very sad.

She pursed her lips. "Awww, poor baby. C'mon, I know it's Sunday, but I have the key to the city and I can let you in and help you hunt for it."

"You sure? I mean, Ping-Pong with the mayor is a wild game — that thing could've whipped anywhere...." Like in his fucking closet or in his damn drawer.

We strolled good-naturedly to the town hall. Her laughter rang as she told me a funny-to-her story about her dog and the post man. Her words were like bee-buzz in my ears as I wondered how in the world I was going to find 'magic tea' in the mayor's office while pretending to search for a non-existent cufflink. Sigh. Ghost busting wasn't easy work. She rattled her key in the lock of the office door and made the frosty glass in the door shake with the effort. Cold air met us when we walked into the empty room — tax payer's money being fed to the AC. We headed straight for the mayor's door, which she unlocked with another key.

She walked over to the Ping-Pong table.

I made a straight line for his desk.

She crawled under the table. "It's probably over here somewhere — dontcha' think?"

"Mmmm...I don't know...I think I might have flicked my wrist like this," I made a big show of demonstrating my exceptional Ping-Pong backhand, "which caused it to fling over here." I indicated the general desk area.

She lay on the carpet and licked her ice cream under the Ping-Pong table. "Are you secretly in here searching for something else?"

I shuffled through the shit on his desktop. Pet rock, stained coffee cup with dregs in it, Mad Libs, official-looking paperwork that probably wasn't, elastics.... "Yes. You're right. I'm searching for the liquid crack tea that your boss buys from old lady Franklin."

She laughed and came out from under the table. "What in the hell do you want that for?"

I opened one drawer after another and didn't find shit. "Your boss is a prick and I'm trying to catch him on something."

"Roving-hands-Ronald — a prick? Surely, you jest." She unlocked his cabinet and started rifling through the contents. "There's no tea in here."

I slammed the last drawer shut. "Great. There's nothing in these drawers, either. He must keep it at home." I checked out her smokin' hot, old-lady-body and gave her the eye. "You sure you don't drink the magic tea, too?"

"Screw you." She folded her arms across her chest and challenged me with the evil eye. "I work very, *very* hard to look like this."

"And you're absolutely gorgeous."

I caught her off guard. She blushed and walked over to the desk to stand beside me. "Anything?"

"No, there's nothing here." I sat on his over-stuffed leather chair.

She wrinkled her nose. "Vile man — he never cleans his cup. Be right back." She picked up his coffee mug and hesitated. She sniffed the contents. She peered inside. "Mr. Park, do you think *this* is the magic tea?" She sniffed the stuff again and balked.

I reached for it, and sniffed it when she gave it to me. I detected the familiar scent of shoe leather and grass. I considered the floaties in the brown liquid. "Do you have something I can transport this in?"

She went in the main room for a minute then returned with a Ziploc snack bag. "Here, try this...I don't know...."

I poured the liquid in the bag then locked the zip. I tipped the bag very carefully. Nothing leaked out. I gave her two thumbs up. "We're good."

Chapter 18

She locked both doors behind us as we left the mayor's office. We marched straight out the lobby doors, down the granite steps and ten yards down the street to the police station. When we entered the station, I was shocked. Where I live in New Mexico, we've got some big-ass police stations. Sprawling things that consume many levels and many square miles. The Peachtree police station was made up of one big room, that's it, a la Mayberry R.F.D. There were six desks in front of us, lined up in neat little rows.

Beyond them, four jail cells lined the back wall — two right against the back of the wall and two coming forward on each side of the room.

The mayor's assistant marched up to the first desk where the only officer in the room was busy studying at his computer screen. It looked like he was wearing the concentrating-hard-on-solitaire face, but hey, I can't be sure. He closed the screen before we could see what he was doing. He feigned boredom, but couldn't keep his eyes off the assistant's mouth when he said, "What do you want, Yvette?"

"Police Chief Radner, I expect a certain amount of decorum — I'm here on official business."

He didn't take his eyes off her. His expression changed from boredom to resignation. And, I didn't know what in the world was passing back and forth between those two, but I suddenly felt very bad for the police chief. He picked up a pile of papers and shuffled them. "How can I be of service?"

Yvette elbowed me. I pulled the tea sample out of my pocket. "We have reason to believe there's drug trafficking going on in your town of a substance that may be illegal and is certainly harmful."

The chief took the sample. He opened the bag and sniffed. "Where did you get this?"

Yvette grunted. "From the mayor's coffee cup." She rolled her eyes.

The chief sat back in his cheap roller chair. "Shit, Yvette, again? I can't use this as evidence — it wasn't obtained legally. How do I know where you two got this? How can you prove he was drinking it?"

"Derek, give me a break. You know Ronald...."

"Yeah, I know he's smart enough not to get caught. Say I believe you," he addressed her then pointed at me, "which is a bloody long shot" And you, "I heard about your outburst at the diner today, and you're under arrest by the way" Then back at Yvette, "You can't just break into his office and collect a sample."

I jumped back and my Stetson fell over my eyes. "What? Under arrest? For talking in a restaurant?"

"Derek! I didn't *break into* his office! He gave me a key!"

He ignored her. "You're under arrest for disturbing the peace." Then back at Yvette again, "You can't just go take evidence willy-nilly. There's procedure that must be followed or we'll lose this non-existent case in court!" He stood up and took his gen-u-ine Barney Fife keychain off of his belt hook. "Now, you, come with me and get in this cell."

Yvette tugged on his arm as he walked me to the cell. "Derek, please, you know I'm right. We didn't know it was the tea before! Now we know! And we know who else is probably using the stuff! And we certainly know who's making it!"

He pushed me into the cell. "Oh, leave that weird old lady alone."

Yvette leaned on my cell bars. "And you know he's got his kid picking it up. You just know he does! Shit! It all makes sense now."

I leaned my face on the bars. "Hey, you two...I know some of what you're talking about, and I can guess at a lot more..."

The chief gave me a warning look.

"...I know, I know — you don't want to hear about my guesses. I have actual proof about something horrid that's going on. And Pamela Franklin is the cause of this horribleness, but in a way I could never prove. So, ah, you need to get her on the drug charges so the horribleness can stop." I took my Stetson off and raked my hand through my hair.

The chief inspected me like a little kid he was extremely disappointed in.

I took a deep breath. "I found bones. I can tell they're human."

"Ah, shit." The chief spun around and stalked back to his desk. He picked up a CB. "Where the hell are these bones, Mr. Park?"

I described the section of woods as best I could.

"What? The woods near Old Crabapple Road?"

I shrugged.

He spoke into the mouthpiece, ordered a unit to the area. He clicked off and zeroed in on me. "Yeah, you won't be going anywhere for a while."

***

I sat in that jail for days. No one told me what was going on, but there was a lot of kafuffle in the office, and I felt a high energy that turned me into a raving insomniac.

On the third day, the Chief came up to my cell waving the key ring. "If I let you out, to talk man-to-man, you gonna give me any trouble?"

I was sitting on my bunk, trimming my toenails. The bathroom in the station had a couple of shower stalls where I could clean up, under watch, so I was fresh and clean. "I think you're pretty safe from me." I held the nail clippers out. "You want my weapon?"

The chief grimaced. "Put that shit down and get out here."

We walked to his desk. There were two Styrofoam take-out containers there — I saw a deputy bring them in a little earlier. The chief pushed one to me. "You eat chicken parm?"

That made me all a quiver. "I love chicken parm!" It was good too — all gooey and crispy and warm. The curly fries were getting cold, but I didn't care. I was still very thankful I wanted to eat *them* and not the guy who fried them.

The Chief said, "So, tell me your whole story. I want to hear it — what you actually saw, and what you speculate. Let's go — give it to me."

I told him everything. You should have seen his face when I said things like, 'demon,' 'possessed,' and 'I wanted to eat her.'

Deputy Dip yelled over from the next desk, "Yee haw! Who didn't want to eat Angel Fairlee?"

The sheriff pointed at him. "You — go do something somewhere else."

The deputy took off with a grumble and a nasty word for me.

After I finished my sandwich and my story, the Chief put me back in my cell without a word.

On the first day, when Yvette and I had come with our tale, all of the deputies were called in for a meeting. When they went into a small, evidently soundproofed room to have this meeting, I heard the chief tell them that no deputy was to talk to me alone. That he, the chief, was to witness all conversations that I had with anyone, and that those conversations must be recorded. I didn't hear any more after that because they shut the door. So, I was surprised one night, when the young deputy — the one they called Scratch — approached my cell while he was on watch. We were alone in the room. We were used to keeping ourselves busy with magazines, books and games. He played a lot of solitaire. He played a radio for us, too — he was my favorite babysitter.

He brought a folding chair with him as he approached my cell. "Can't sleep again, huh?"

I got up and walked over to the bars, ready to talk. The silence was killing me more than the confinement was. "Yeah, you know how it is."

"Yeah." He nodded his head, folded his hands on his lap and stared at me.

I nodded back and stared at him.

He tipped his chair back and spoke to the ceiling. "You, know..." He set the chair back on the ground and went silent.

I gave him a macho man chin-thrust to encourage him to speak. "What's that?"

"I seen that black ghost-fog once."

"You want to talk about that, do you?" I nodded my head. "Okay." Then I returned to bunk, propped my pillow against the concrete wall, and shifted around" "Go ahead."

"Okay, so, it was a coupl'a months back — around Christmas." He snorted, twiddled his fingers. "I was out splittin' wood. I just had a fight with my girlfriend who's not my girlfriend anymore and I needed to blow off steam, ya know?"

So, he needed to take an ax to something when he got mad at his girlfriend — interesting. It was probably a good thing they weren't together anymore. "Oh, yeah, yeah — I know what you mean, man."

"Yeah, and I was out there choppin' and choppin' when suddenly I didn't feel right. Like, I felt sick and then right after that, I felt like I was surrounded by the black fog, and it was, I don't know, it was trying to open my mouth or something. Since I felt like it was doin' that, I didn't open my mouth and I covered it right up with both hands and ran to the house."

Sigh. Why didn't *I* think of that?

"I only knew to do that because there was already talk goin' round town, especially here at the station, that the black smoke was goin' around doin' that and the only way to deal with it was to hold your mouth and run away."

Yeah, that was a good talk with him. He gave me important information that I could have benefitted from had it been in the welcome kit. But since my welcome kit was from the mayor....

On day five — or was it day eight — important-looking hard-asses with DEA jackets came into the station and shuffled into the soundproofed room — but not before they all got a good, long look at me.

That night, Scratch came over with a box of Twizzlers. "Hey, Sebastian, they got enough on the old lady! They're gonna bring her in! Turns out there was coke in that tea!" He hooted and slapped his knee. "Coke — can you believe it? Besides that, there were seven other 'unidentified substances'." He made the quote symbols with his fingers, then handed me a wad of Twizzlers. He munched. "*And*, they found stuff in that room off her kitchen, stuff you wouldn't believe, like boxes and boxes of herbs. And nobody knew what any of it was. They had to send it all out to be identified. And there was like, voodoo dolls or something, and other weird shit, man."

I was glad to have some news, but oh, how I wished to read an official report.

They brought Pamela in the next morning. She walked slowly to her cell, with a deputy holding each elbow and her beautiful daughter trailing behind. The daughter wouldn't acknowledge me. Her face was puffy and tear-streaked.

Mrs. Franklin smiled at me as she slow-walked.

They took a long time making sure she was comfortable and set up in her cell. Clearly, there were still some who didn't believe my entire story. They probably thought I had caused the capture of a sweet little drug lord. Her daughter stayed with her for a long time. They sat on the bunk together and whispered.

Hours later, the girl came over to my cell. "You're a horrible man — she trusted you! Why couldn't you leave her alone? She was just giving people what they wanted. Did you know that the herbs in that tea hadn't been used in centuries? Fantastic herbs that actually slowed down the process of aging.... People think she's amazing — a wonder women! She wasn't hurting people – she was helping them! But, oh no, here you come with the stinking DEA to suppress something else you don't know about. And because you don't know about it, you're afraid of it! Now, they'll just lock those herbs up and study them for a hundred years and make sure no one can benefit from them. You should be ashamed of yourself!"

It made me sad to watch her beautiful face as she stared at me with hate. I wanted to tell her so badly what her mother really was. That her mother had given birth to her and sent her away for the sole purpose of calling her back and harvesting her body. But I couldn't say that — she would never, ever believe me. So I just let myself float in her angel eyes for a moment and said nothing until she turned to walk away.

"You're welcome." I called out.

She chucked me the bird.

I glared at Mrs. Franklin. I was suddenly zapped with electricity and it hurt like a bitch.

She grinned. "You like that?"

I got my hands off the cell bars before she did it again. I think it took the piss out of her to do it because her shoulders were suddenly sagging. "What the hell did you just do?"

She shrugged. "You can't touch me, Mr. Park."

I made sure I didn't appear impressed. "I already know that."

She nodded slowly. "Of course you do."

I perked up, "You can rot in jail, though, can't you?"

She gave a barking laugh. "Well, maybe...but that could take awhile. My good girl is going to work on my defense. My good girl is going to try and raise funds for my bail." She sighed. "You know, you haven't done this town a bit of good. Now they will all be prey. There will be no one to tell me about the criminals that hide in and pass through

Peachtree. And if I'm stuck in here," she indicated the cell bars, "there will be no way to guide those nasty people to their destiny.... They will be free to roam and rape, to rob and steal babies, to burn and destroy. Do you think people will thank you for that?" She shook her head slowly. "I don't think they'll thank you, Mr. Park. Why do you think things have gone on the same way in Peachtree as long as they have? For centuries.... Because the people *liked* the service I provided for them. No one likes to discuss the dirty work, Mr. Park, but everyone appreciates it. Now the filth and shit will run free in this town just like every other town in the world. And people will suffer." She lay back on her bunk and said no more.

I admit. I was stunned into silence. The deputy leaned back in his rolly chair and gave me the 'what a fruitcake' look. But I knew she wasn't a fruitcake. I knew she was a frightening and effective tool. Dangerous.

Yvette came flowing into the station in a silk tunic, smelling like expensive perfume and carrying a bunch of flowers, a bag of chips, and a diet soda. She waggled her fingers at the deputy. He gave her a wink. She never quite closed her mouth as she chewed her gum and her shiny teeth sparkled.

I rubbed my lips together. "You sure you weren't drinking that miracle tea?"

"Oh, you; just stop it now. "I drink Rooibos — it's miracle enough. Here..." Through the bars, she handed me the flowers, chips, and soda. She took two small plastic cups from her coat pocket. "Pour out, we're celebrating." After I poured hers, I handed it over.

"What are we celebrating, exactly?"

She chewed her gum faster. "Well, first of all, Roving-Hands-Ronald is locked up! You have no idea how long I've been waiting for them to pin something, *something* on him — he was the most loathsome, most corrupt man I had ever met! And nobody could catch him at anything! The town was totally split down the middle on who loved him and who hated him. The people who loved him didn't really know him. All they cared about was the fact that he was the mayor of the town with the lowest crime rate in America. And the people that hated him, hated him because they were afraid of him. And you won't believe it — you know Patricia Swasky that works out on I-89 at the welcome center? Well, you probably don't know her, but..."

"Yeah, I know her." I raised my eyebrows and widened my eyes to indicate that I thought Patricia Swasky was a real lulu.

"...Yeah, right! Well, she was buying the tea wholesale and reselling it to other people! Can you believe that? Patricia-tight-ass-Swasky — Drug Dealer!" She clapped her hands with glee. "And they arrested a whole boatload of other people in town." She named a ton of names, some of which I was vaguely familiar with, and even more that I hadn't heard before. "They had to bring in a paddy wagon and transport them all to another town because this facility wasn't big enough to hold them all!"

The chief came into the office. He jerked his thumb at the door. "C'mon, Yvette, out — I've got business to go over with your party boy."

Yvette scrunched her nose at me. She put her face close to the bars and offered me her cheek. I kissed it, then she offered the other cheek. "Okay, sweetheart. I just want to thank you — you've done this town a lot of good. I'll swing by the inn later, around dinner."

When she mentioned Rog, my heart fell to my cowboy boots — I had just caused the arrest of his girlfriend. Was I even allowed back in his house? He was probably gonna kill me.

The chief unlocked my door. "Get your stuff; after we talk, you're free to go."

"Oh!" I yelled and quickly threw out my trash, collected my things and set my Stetson atop my mop.

I met him at his desk. "Thanks, Derek."

"I'm not comfortable with you calling me Derek." He took a coffee mug out of his drawer and waggled it at his deputy.

"Okay then, thank you, Chief."

"You're welcome. I've got some questions."

The door opened behind me and several FBI agents piled in. The chief pointed to the soundproofed room. "I'll be with you in a couple of minutes. I'm just finishing up with Mr. Park, then we can get on with it." He eyed the deputy when the lad returned with his coffee. "And you will process Mr. Park when I'm done so he can get the hell out."

The deputy saluted. "Aye, aye, Captain!"

The Chief flipped through the paperwork in front of him and mumbled, "Watch yourself, Deputy," without conviction. To me he said, "So, you're off the hook, Mr. Park.

There are no charges against you and you are no longer a person of interest." He pointed at my face — he really liked to point. "However, we may still have questions for you, so stick around for a few days."

I nodded amicably. "Yes, sir."

"I want you to know that you will be getting paid for your investigative time."

"Really?" *That* was shocking.

"Yes, sir, I made sure of that myself. You've done this town a real service." He leaned on the desk and considered me for a long time. "We found the bones you mentioned. We found them the first day."

I leaned forward, too, and rested my elbows on my knees. "Whoa."

"Yes, 'whoa'. Of course I can't go into any great detail, evidence pending and all, but I can tell you, we know who the murderer is — we've got hair samples, skin samples, saliva samples — a sample buffet — evidence everywhere. We know who it is, it's just a matter of time before we track him down."

I chuckled without humor. "Oh, I see — you think you're after some guy...some human." I put my face in my hands. "You don't really think you're after a demon wearing some poor idiot's skin, do you...."

He frowned hard. "No, Mr. Park, we do not."

I leaned back and sighed. "Okay. Fine. Can I go now?"

He stood up, and reached across the desk to shake my hand. As he walked towards the soundproofed room he snapped, "Process Mr. Park, Deputy."

Chapter 19

I had a plan.

That last squirrelly Indian I met, Long-Feather, told me I had to trap the monster and pray the shit out of it, just like they did to get that little bit out of monster out of me — and I had a plan. But first, I had to face Roger.

When I pulled into his driveway, I was shocked to see that the entire parking area was empty. Rog had a very popular B&B and, up until that point, I had never seen his driveway without a few cars parked in it. When I ducked inside, I found him sitting at his big, empty dining table. His eyes were red as if he'd been crying.

Uh-oh. I took off my Stetson and held it to my chest. "Hey there, buddy."

He used both hands to play with the edge of the tablecloth. "Hi, Casper." His voice was flat.

"Can I come and sit with you?" I was ready to run.

"Sit wherever the Sam Hill you wanna sit." He flung the tablecloth away from him and wiped at his eyes.

"Sorry about Pamela, Rog."

"You sorry she's a drug dealer, or you sorry you got her locked up?"

"I'm sorry you're in love with an evil woman, and I'm sorry I had to be the one to expose her."

To my surprise, he started laughing. Well, he started shaking and making that noise people make when you're not sure if they're crying or laughing. I wasn't any good with hysteria.

"Boy, I always knew she was an evil woman..." he held his hands up in defense, "...well, not *that* evil...but a wild and wicked woman all the same. I've known her ever since she moved to Peachtree, don't forget. I helped her out when she was newly reunited with her momma and then lost her momma so suddenly."

I was so sick of hearing that tale. Now my voice was flat. "Uh-huh."

"After her momma's death, she just spiraled out of control. Started sleeepin' around with everyone in three counties." He put a hand to his chest. "Oh, how that hurt my heart. I was so in love with that girl and she just ran around and around and around." He gave me imploring eyes. "But I had to understand, she grew up an orphan —which is never easy — then she's finally reunited with her momma and the poor old lady dies."

I cleared my throat. "Yeah, about that..."

274

He shook his head and closed his eyes. "Oh, no you won't, Casper. I don't want to hear what you got to say yet. You just listen to me."

I sighed loudly.

"You don't know what it's like. I know you had your momma and your daddy – I listened well to your stories. You gotta understand — this girl had no momma and daddy to lovingly show her the ropes in life. So, she finally gets word that she *has* a momma and when she gets up here, she loses the woman all over again!" He suddenly turned, and yelled at the swinging kitchen door, "Travis! Bring us some vittles!"

He made me jump.

"Sorry about that. Anyway, she got pregnant from all her running around. I heard she was planning on giving the baby up. I went over, one time, and begged her not to do the same that her momma had done to her. I implored her to remember the pain she felt, but she wouldn't be moved. You know how it is — the apple doesn't fall far from the tree."

"Yeah, what if the apple and the tree are the same plant?"

"Shut up, boy — I don't have any patience for your funny talk today."

I put my head down on my arms and suffered the rest of his speech.

"Over the years, she was into other, secretive stuff that I suspected wasn't on the up-and-up, but I didn't see any evidence of any harm done. As the years went on, she started accepting my help and we developed a relationship of sorts." He sniffed. "Best years of my life. But now...she's gone...."

"She's been communing with that black smog — it's a demon — she's been enabling it." Whew! I got it out!

He slapped the table and I jumped again. "Now, I don't want to hear any of that bullshit! You hear me?"

Travis kicked the swinging door open and shuffled over with a tray full of pre-made finger foods.

"Don't kick my door, boy!"

Travis hid behind his bangs and shuffled back.

Rog took a deep breath then released it in a long, decompressing way. "Now, let's just have something to eat and talk about something else, shall we?"

I shrugged. "Whatever you say, Boss."

With his mouth full of food and crumbs pouring forth when he chew-talked, he said, "I heard you're still getting paid. You owe me money."

We knocked our little sandwiches together as if we were toasting.

***

I got up early the next day and ate an omelet, pancakes, and corned beef hash with an appreciative zeal. Rog didn't ask me what I was up to that day. And now that I knew him better, I knew why — he didn't pay too much mind to his friends when they were up to no good. Hey, at least I could depend on him in that way.

Part of my plan involved going back to the cemetery to see the creepy mayor's kid. I think I was a little bit better with him. I felt bad for him — that his father had gone to prison — and I learned to focus on his good eye when I talked to him, so the going wasn't so rough. I found him in his barn, rearranging 'his stuff.' The garage door was wide open, so I walked through it.

"Knock knock."

Al had a doll in his hands. His movements were slow as he stood up, reached for his sports jacket, and wiggled into it. He shuffled over to greet me. "Hey, I remember you! Did you come back to check out my stuff with me?"

I stood up straight and talked perky. "I sure did!"

He crossed his arms over his pudgy belly and stared down at his sneakers. I could hardly hear him as he mumbled, "My dad went to prison." His threadbare cuffs rode all the way up to his elbows.

"Yeah, buddy, I know. It's all right. It's all right." I patted his shoulder and as I did, I noticed my L.L.Bean folding chair just behind him — the one he had removed from my campsite. I walked over to it, picked it up and walked back to where he was standing; it was the only clean spot in the entire barn. Al's cave couldn't hold much more murder booty. "You know, Al..."

He raised his head and there on his face was a big, goofy smile. "You know my name!"

"Yes, I know your name. I also know you're a very nice person. Now, you know that just because your father did something bad that it doesn't mean that *you* are bad...you know that, right?"

"Yeah, that's what my mom said." He strained to sit down on an old tire. "She said people in town might not be nice to me because of my father, and that I had to remember that I'm not my father, even if they forget. She said that I have to remember that I'm a good man."

I nodded. "That's true, that's true. Your mother is a very good woman." If only she didn't drop you in the washing machine.... "Al, I have a job for you, if you want it. I need some work done in the woods. You got a Kubota tractor, right? I saw it parked out front last time I was here."

"Yeah! I drive that tractor!"

"Aw, that's great! Where is it, Al?" All of our talk in expletives was draining.

"It's down the middle, on the edge of the cemetery." He hung his head. "They found Edward Locklin's bones. Everyone thought he went off to be a rockstar with his slut girlfriend, but it just turned out that he was dead."

"Um, Al? You know how you don't want people to hurt your feelings because your father went to prison?"

"Yeah?"

"Well, you shouldn't refer to Eddie's girlfriend as his 'slut girlfriend' because it's not very nice, in the same way."

He frowned. His brow furrowed. His good eye almost crossed over to meet his wayward eye. "Oh."

"Yeah, you can just say, 'Eddie's girlfriend'."

He brightened up again. "Yeah! All right!"

"Al? Can you show me how you can drive the tractor? I have to test you for the first day on the job."

"Sure! Come on!" He took my hand and held it all the way down to the middle of the cemetery.

Fine with me. I just wanted to see him operate that tractor. There was no other man for this job than him — he-who-would-do-anything-without-repeating. And wouldn't you know, he was a real pro. He could move that thing around like it was on rails. And he was fast with it, too — had Eddie's grave dug out in minutes.

He got off the tractor and wiped the sweat off his brow. "How'd I do?"

"That was fantastic, Al!"

He bit his bottom lip. In a hushed voice he said, "I wasn't supposed to dig that till tomorrow."

"Tell them that you forgot about that rule."

"Forgot? I can tell them that?"

"Sure!"

The glow returned to his cheeks. "Okay! I'll tell them that I forgot!"

"Great!" I swung my arm around. "Great! You got a trailer for that thing, right?" He followed me around like a puppy as I helped him prepare the tractor for transport.

By the time we got the Kubota on its trailer, hooked the trailer up to the white pickup, and started driving, it was almost noon. We were on our merry way to Old Crabapple Road — the northern end where most of the bone mounds were found.

There wasn't much traffic on Old Crabapple, so we were able to get the tractor untethered and onto the road without a single car driving by. Al started her up, I climbed on and clung to the frame on the side, and we were off — driving into the woods on my direction. When I showed Al where to stop, he drove to the spot and cut the engine.

I got off the tractor and walked a little away from it. Then I stood there for several long moments, taking deep breaths and sensing my surroundings. I closed my eyes and listened to the sounds of the forest. I let my mind drift. I concentrated on nothing, but let in everything. I heard Canadian geese as they honked in mid-flight. They must've started their migration. Even farther away, I heard the hum of a chainsaw. I smelled the dirt and pine needles beneath my feet. I felt the breeze on my cheek and tasted the air. I soaked up all of these sensations and went with my gut...that thing wasn't here. It wasn't watching us. I opened my eyes, blinked a couple of times and clapped my hands. "Okay, you ready to get started, Al?"

"What are we doing out here, Mr. Sebastian? This part of the forest is haunted." He jumped from one foot to the other as he scanned the woods. He was like a nervous little kid. I felt bad.

"It'll be alright, Al — I'm with you. Do you know what I was just doing?"

He shrugged. "No."

"Well, I was using my senses to see if a monster was around here. I'm working to strengthen my psychic gifts, which means that I'll soon be able to sense things around me that I can't see."

His mouth dropped open. "Wow! That's something!"

"Yes, it is! It is something! My grandmother was very good at it and I think, because I'm related to her, I can get very good at it, too. I didn't believe in any of it till I came to your town. Now I'm going to use it to help a lot of people."

"And you will too! I can tell!"

I blushed and looked down at my boots. All this truth-telling and honest magic-man talk was a little bit embarrassing for me.

He thumbed his chest and looked victorious. "Because I can see colors. Pardon me, but when you first came into my barn, your color was dirty."

That got my attention. "What do you mean, 'colors'?"

He moved his hands around my body like he was shaping the air to me. "Like the color all around you — it's blue, like the ocean." He patted my back. "It's not dirty anymore. You're much better now."

I busted out laughing. "Well, *that's* good to know! You little dickens, Al! C'mon — we need to dig a big hole here." I pointed. "You can even make it bigger than the holes you make at the cemetery!"

His eyes shined and he was all teeth. "Really?!"

This kid was too funny — he made me want to smile, too. "Really!"

He actually swung his fist like a Little Rascal. "Well, then — let's get to it!"

I walked around the tractor as he worked — making sure the hole was deep without it getting too wide. It was slow going because there were a lot of boulders. Some of them were almost too big to move, but that crafty kid did it. As they came up, I had Al push them off to the side and keep going. The excess dirt we spread out and pulled into the woods so we could camouflage the site later. It was late afternoon by the time the digging was done. It was rectangular-shaped, maybe three coffins wide, almost twenty feet deep, with sheer up and down dirt walls.

"What are you going to do with that hole, Mr. Sebastian?"

"Hopefully, we'll trap the monster in there. That'll keep its body in one place — well, the body it stole." I pulled the sack of salt out of my t-shirt. "Then I'll use this salt to make a ring around the hole. That'll trap the demon inside the body. If it wants to escape, the only way it'll be able to get away is to go to another world. We'll force it out of this world."

"Oh." Al frowned. He lowered his eyebrows and scratched behind his ear. "Is that very nice?"

I jerked my head back. "What? Is what very nice? Is it very nice to get rid of the demon?" My voice was getting shrill. "Ah, yeah...."

"No, no, no, Mr. Sebastian — is it very nice to send it to a different world? What if it hurts the people over there?"

Well, shit. I had no good answer for that. "I hear what you're sayin' buddy, but I don't know what to tell ya. All I know is we have to get rid of this thing."

"Okay," Al said. He sounded like a little kid resigned to go to bed when he still wanted to stay up.

Ai yi yi.

I then explained to Al that I needed to camouflage the top of the hole and began to show him how I wanted it done.

He watched me for five minutes then said, "Mr. Sebastian, that's not how you camouflage a hole — anyone would know that's a hole underneath there — even a monster."

I put my hands on my hips. Sweat ran in my eyes as I studied my shoddy handiwork. "Ya think?" I groaned. "Can you do it any better?"

He used both his hands to push at my arm as he walked past me. "Why, sure! I used to go hunting with my uncles — they taught me all kinds of stuff."

And when that kid was done, you could *not* tell a great big hole was there — it was truly artful.

Chapter 20

Back at the Ox Blood Inn, Rog served me dinner. I

refer to it as my 'last supper.' It was a truly glorious meal, his

culinary expertise was at a peak, and his table was full. The

only reason guests weren't around the day before was

because all of the previous guests had checked out. Now, the

new crop had checked in and Rog was using the same old

tricks he always used to get them settled into the meal and

talking to each other like they were all already friends. I was

unusually quiet that night and savored each and every bite of the butternut squash bisque, roasted pork with chutney, parmesan couscous, and hot apple pie with fresh cream. Brought a tear to my eye, it did. I slept well that night. In the morning, I set out to check my trap.

The site was eerily quiet when I arrived. Although I didn't feel the beast around me, I was still hopeful. I approached the hole slowly. There wasn't a sound. I lifted several sticks — no hole. I was confused — I thought maybe the thing had somehow bested us and filled the hole over night. But no, this dirt was hard-packed — there was never any hole there.

Shit.

I stood up and spun around in a full circle. I could have sworn I was in the right spot. Where was that hole? Twenty feet away from where I stood there was another familiar-looking pine. Was it behind *that* tree? It didn't seem right, but I decided to go check, just to be sure. I took one step, and suddenly, there was no ground beneath my foot where there should have been. I did a discombobulated free-fall for only a second, then — smack — fell on my face. As I groaned, I rolled over on my back and stared at the pine tops and the blue sky way above me. I had knocked a lot of leaves and sticks down with me and the dust from all of the debris whirled around the top of the hole.

Great.

None of the sticks that fell in with me were big enough for me to use to get out of the hole. Of course not — we'd thought of that. I couldn't even use one to scratch at the dirt. Why was I in this hole? Why was that thing not in this hole? It was about 7 a.m. — I had all day to figure out how I was going to get out. I begin to dig at one of the perpendicular walls. Al was a whiz kid — he had dug the hole so that all of the walls were sheer and straight all the way up. I figured I needed to start digging at one of the walls. I'd have to do it for a couple of hours if I was going to bring down enough dirt to build myself up higher and create a slant in the earth that I could crawl out of. I scratched at the wall, but it wasn't topsoil that I was dealing with — that nice, soft, loamy stuff made with fallen leaves and pine needles. No, this was far down, compacted earth, made of clay and rock. I scraped at it a couple of times and split the skin from my fingernail on my middle finger. I gathered a couple of sticks together and used them to scrape, but they kept snapping or wearing down too quickly. I scraped with the fingers of one hand and the wadded up sticks in my other hand, switching back and forth to let the pain ease in my fingers.

I tried using the toe of my boot to kick at the dirt, but it was slow going and hurt like hell. It wasn't long before my bad ankle began to throb. I turned around and around in the hole, studying the dirt. Was there a less-hard area to dig in? Then I saw a spot that was a different color — a darker patch of dirt with yellow pine needles sticking out of it. I reached up to scrape at it and found that it *was* easier to scratch at, so I began jabbing at the spot with my wad of sticks. It did give pretty easily too — dirt started to rain on my head as soon as I began stabbing at the spot. A splash of dirt sprayed in my eyes, but I kept working at the earth with one hand while I pressed on the pain in my eyelids with the other hand. Stab, stab, stab and even more dirt rained down. Big chunks of dirt just rolled out and bounced off my head as I kept stabbing with my eyes closed. Then all of a sudden, I heard a shifting noise. There was a moment of silence, then a 'whoosh' sound of falling dirt and rattling sticks. I got one eye open just as a skull came flying at my face. I ducked to the side and watched a waterfall of bones pour from the side of my hole. At my feet were long femurs and more skulls and fractured arm bones, and little bones that make up your hands and feet. The avalanche left an abscess in the wall big enough for my entire body to fit in. I wanted to shrink into the fetal position and tuck myself in there to hide. These were old, dried out bones, cleaned of all tissue and wet matter and buried a long, long time ago.

As my eyes watered, I reached up and kept pulling the dirt down from the bottom of that hole. My arms were burning. A nerve pinched up in my right shoulder and I began to work slower as all of the effects of working with my arms above my head began to take a toll on my effort. I dug slower then kept digging above me while I hung my head to try and ease the nagging pains going from my shoulder to my neck. Most of the sensation had left my bloody fingertips, so at first, I didn't know I was scratching at a boulder. When I looked up, there was a rock just above me — about twice the size of my head. I began to clean off its sides. Soon, the newly exposed edges of the rock were marred with blood. When it was mostly excavated, I pulled at it. No way — that thing was solidly packed into the wall. The sun was high overhead and hot as it beat down on me. Of course we had dug the hole right where there was no tree shade. Had I known I was going to be such an ignoramus and fall into my own trap, I would have surely built the thing where there was bountiful tree canopy. I pulled at the belly of my filthy t-shirt and wiped all the sweat and dirt off my face, then went back to work excavating the boulder. About half an hour later, I was able to get both of my hands on each side of the boulder. The top was mostly cleaned off, and I assumed that I should be able to wiggle it out. I braced myself by putting one foot against the wall in front of me and I stretched my other leg behind me to bear the brunt of my weight. I pulled and shoved at the rock. At first, it wouldn't budge. So I pushed and shoved harder, until I felt it move forward just a little. Then it moved more and more. I felt it scooting forward. I put my foot higher up on the wall, grabbed the rock harder and pulllllllllled.

I didn't know the shape of the rock. I didn't know it had no rear end on it. I thought it was a big, round boulder and would take a certain amount of pulling weight to get it out. I was wrong. The boulder was flat on the back end. It was stuck in the dirt not because it was heavy, but because it was awkwardly shaped. When the last bit of anchoring dirt gave way, the rock easily popped forward, smashed me in the forehead, and knocked me out cold.

When I woke up, it was dark. I had a piercing eyeball headache and my eyes stayed out of focus for several minutes after I opened them. I was lying in the pile of bones. When I turned my head I found a skull there, laughing at me. I sat up with a groan as the hole whirled round and round me. I shook as I got to my knees and felt nauseous as I lurched to my feet. I couldn't stop swaying as I walked over to the hole I'd made in my hole. I began scratching.

***

Al was very afraid. He had ridden his bike on Old Crabapple Road at night plenty of times, but tonight was different. The color around him had changed, which meant something wasn't right, and as he left the bike on the side of the road and started walking in the forest, he was afraid. He didn't need a flashlight, the full moon helped him find his way, and he knew exactly where the hole was. He hoped his new friend wasn't in trouble. He whispered to himself, over and over again, 'please let him be alright.' He had been hunting for Mr. Sebastian all day. He asked everyone in town. Mrs. Franklin wasn't home. He liked Mr. Sebastian. Mr. Sebastian was the most beautiful color. He hadn't been this afraid when they took his father away. His father had always been a dirty, dull color. His mother's color had improved since his father had been in jail, so he decided jail was a good place for his father.

He stepped through the forest with almost no sound as all. Briars didn't pull on his clothes and jutting branch arms didn't catch him in the face. He had walked these woods hundreds of times. He knew the monster was around.

He could smell him. He was used to the monster's smell; it was always there when he found the treasures. His father had always told him to take all of the treasures he found, every little bit, and the monster wouldn't get him if he did a good job cleaning up. He had seen the monster once as it had run away. He was tall and very bony and he had no color around him. Al had never seen a creature without color. This lack of color made Al's breath come too fast, so fast sometimes, that he wanted to lie down and stop breathing all together. But his father told him it was his job to do the clean up — even if he felt like he couldn't breathe — so Al did it.

As Al got closer to Monster Graveyard, the monster's smell grew stronger. Was the monster in the hole? Al hunched over and tiptoed into the clearing. The moon lit the entire space and showed him that the big, gaping hole he had made wasn't covered with his camouflage anymore. He got down on his hands and knees and crawled to the edge of the hole. He shrieked and covered his mouth. Mr. Sebastian was down there! Mr. Sebastian was digging real fast and crying like a baby. He was wiping his snots on his shirt like a baby, too. Mr. Sebastian's color was run through with lightning bolts, which meant he was really, really scared — probably more scared than he, himself, was.

***

I heard a noise above me, like the squeal of a small animal being strangled. I looked up, expecting to see that thing, biting the head off a rodent. But no, it was Al — beautiful Al — with his fat, cherubic face and his roly-poly eye. "Oh, my God, Al. Oh, my God." I tottered then, and almost crashed to the ground in exhaustion and relief.

Al was shaking his head. "No, Mr. Sebastian, it's not okay, yet." He lowered his voice and hissed, "The monster is around here. You have to hide!" Suddenly, he looked to his left.

My voice came out high and hysterical. "Are you kidding me, Al? Hide?" I made fists with both hands and started pummeling the dirt walls. "Where am I supposed to hide!?"

In a loud whisper he said, "You have to get out of there. It's coming!"

He turned his head to his right, then back at me. Then over to his right again, and back at me. Then he got up and walked away, for the love of Pete! I thought my eyes would pop out of my head. I put my mouth on my arm to stifle the little noises of panic that I couldn't stop from pealing out of me. For the first time in my life, I actually tasted fear — it's like the copper flavor you get in your nose when you're drowning, except it also has this aftertaste of steel. As if the steel is electrified and zapping your tongue over and over again.

I inspected the hole that I'd made inside the hole I ordered to be made. I had scratched enough at the bottom —

I could reach up and pull myself in there. I grabbed at the lip of the hole and pulled myself up, scrambling like a cartoon character, as I struggled to make my slippery cowboy boots gain purchase with the smooth dirt wall. With all of my muscles screaming and my fractured bones splintering, I got into the small hole, curled into the fetal position and stuffed the neck of my t-shirt into my mouth, backed by both fists.

I was about to be eaten alive.

I realized I was an idiot, and that I shouldn't have done this. I should've left town. I should've left town a long time ago and left Peachtree alone. If I had not come, maybe Angel wouldn't be dead. Maybe only bad people would be dead. I was breathing too fast. I couldn't stop breathing like that. My head was swimming. My vision was blurring. I was soaked with sweat and I couldn't stop breathing like that. Why did Al leave me?

Then I heard that thing up there. I heard its breaths — deep and phlegmy — and I smelled its reeking-like-

301

rotting-shit putrid stench. I tucked myself in tighter and held my breath. It stood there forever, stinking and breathing. Then there was a silence I didn't understand until two horrible seconds later, when I realized the thing had gone quiet because it was in mid-air. It had jumped into the pit.

It landed two feet in front of me. Its head was at the same height as mine as I lay frozen stiff in my hole. It hadn't seen me yet; it was facing the wrong direction. There was plenty of moonlight and it filled the hole, illuminating the nightmare the wheezed and quivered not four feet away from me. On the back of its head was peeling, yellow, waxy skin. There was a noise from above, a dark shadow, and suddenly the creature wasn't there anymore. I pulled my shirt out of my mouth and stretched my head out of the hole. I pulled my head back into the hole when the awful screaming started. It was a garbled scream of rage that made my eardrums pop. I stretched my head out again and looked down. There below me, pinned to the ground and surrounded by human bones, lay the thing. A huge boulder lay on its middle. I could see the massive weight of the stone had caused its ribs to snap. The splintered edges of bone had torn through its thin skin and were poking out, glistening in the moonlight. It thrashed its arms and legs and threw its head from side to side. It had no ears, no nose and was missing some fingers. Skin was scraped off to the bone on its elbows and knees. Most of the hair was gone. It screamed and screamed. It wore no clothing. Under the rock I could see where a penis had fallen off.

Its eyes moved back and forth several times at an impossible speed then rested on me. Shit. I fumbled as I yanked the salt pouch out of my t-shirt. I reached out and sprinkled the salt all around it while I mumbled, "Dear God, let this salt trap that demon in its circle. Dear God, let this salt trap that demon in its circle. It wasn't a perfect circle — I was shaking so much, and the confines of the hole were so narrow that some of the salt sprinkled on the body. Every time the salt hit it, I could hear popping and sizzling. The skin on the thing started to smoke, and soon enough the hole was filled with the stench of burning hair as well as the stench of rotten flesh and infection. After I had chanted 'Dear God let this salt trap that demon in its circle,' twenty or thirty times, I started chanting, 'Please, God, let your white light surround me and protect me. All of you souls near me — please help me,' over and over and over.

The thing had slowed its thrashing, but it still squirmed as it said, "You will come here to me and give me your body. That is my body. Eat the boy! Eat the boy!"

I heard Al shriek and yell, "Please don't eat me, Mr. Sebastian!" from somewhere up top. He was still up there. So it must've been him — he must have pushed the big rock onto the thing.

I yelled out, "I'm not going to eat you, Al," then jabbed a finger at the spasmodic body, "And you will shut the hell up." I shook with fear as I said it, but I was also indignant. I was sick of its shit. "See? I've protected myself, I have people here to help me, and I have trapped you in that salt. We are sick of your crap, and we want you to get out. You cannot stay here on Earth anymore. You go somewhere else, and you're never invited back to Peachtree, ever again. Or anywhere else around here." I thought. "Yeah, or anywhere on Earth. Leave now!" From my hole, where I still lay crunched up, I flicked my hand at it.

It roared in rage. Its eyes rolled around and around. They turned black, like shiny onyx marbles. "You cannot banish me! You are no one!" It rocked back and forth and flailed its limbs. It did a sit up and hissed at me.

I screamed, pulled my head back into my hole, and yelled, "Get out! Get out! Get out! I banish you!" Then repeated that about a hundred times as it swore at me.

It ripped one of its arms off and threw it at me as it screamed, "Eat the boy! Eat the boy! Eat the boy!" in a garbled demon lisp.

If I hadn't been sure of myself before, I was now. There was no way I was going to eat Al. Not even tempting. I was starting to realize that I could defeat that thing. We volleyed back and forth a few times, it was swearing, I was threatening it with God — and getting real forceful and loud about it — when I realized it was thrashing far less and its voice was weakening. It still stank like fat-fold cheese, but I was thrilled — it was weakening.

I looked up. "Hey, Al?" The thing was spewing black sludge and choking on it. I saw Al's face pop into view at the top of the hole.

"Yeah, Mr. Sebastian?"

"Do you know any prayers?"

"Yes, Sir! Lots!"

I shifted and made sure I got both of my hands in his view. I gave him two thumbs up. "That's great, buddy! Can you say all the prayers you know over and over again?"

"Sure!" And he began by saying "Our Father, who art in heaven...."

Such a sweet kid.

The slobbering mess jerked around on the floor of the hole. "I banish you from here. You have no power here. You have to leave. You can never come back here. You have no power here. I banish you...." And whatever else I could think of along the same lines. In those moments, I knew I'd never pooh-pooh a television evangelist again, because right then, I was that person. I was screaming and yelling and pointing down at that thing. Smiting it with the word of God, and in general, just being a crazed zealot. I was doing it because I *felt* it, I was caught up in the moment and actually felt a power surging through me. It was a power so incredible, I can only describe it as orgasmic. Below me, the body moved less and less, until finally, it moved no more.

With much pain, I wiggled out of my little hole and stood on top of the boulder. At my feet lay the deformed shell of what was once a man. I looked up at Al. "I don't know if it's gone." I looked back down.

Al's voice was rough and crackly, "Yes. It's gone. There's a dirty brown light around that body down there, and it's fading. I think the real guy in that body is about to die because that monster had no light at all." He nodded solemnly.

I smiled up at him. "You're an incredibly useful person, you know that, Al?"

He wiped the sweat off his lip and beamed like a prize winner. We backfilled the hole. I don't know whose body was down there, but the dude shouldn't be remembered as a murderer. It wasn't his fault.

I left Peachtree two days later and never went back. I made a couple of phone calls and found out that Buck was well — he had been in the hospital for days, in a coma and hanging on to life by a thread. Then one night, he suddenly came out of it. His doctor, his family and friends — they had no idea how it happened, but they were all thankful for the miracle.

It was the same night Al and I defeated the demon.

www.ingramcontent.com/pod-product-compliance
Lightning Source LLC
Chambersburg PA
CBHW032207190626
46810CB00019B/2167